I0654597

# Two Images of God

## Conflict

*Brian P. Sheets*

# Two Images of God
## Conflict

Published by:
Priati Publications
6217 E. Empire Ave., Suite 100
Prescott Valley, AZ   86314   USA
www.priatipub.com

**Cover Design**
Karl May, Karl May's Marketing & Media
karl_may@karlmaysmarketingandmedia.com

ISBN 978-0-9971108-7-6

**Limits of Liability and Disclaimer of Warranty**

This book is strictly for informational, educational, and entertainment purposes. The author and publisher shall have neither liability nor responsibility to anyone with respect to any loss or damage caused, or alleged to be caused, directly or indirectly, by the information contained in this book or the reader's misuse of this material.

All prime characters appearing in this work are fictitious. Any resemblance to real persons, living or dead, is purely coincidental.

References to historical incidents were used to lend a degree of authenticity to this fictional work. Any similarities between these incidents and the characters in this book are coincidental.

References to actual historical personages, assets, and locations have been taken from publicly available sources. Use of such historical information has been done to provide background context for the reader to better understand the story. There is no actual relationship between historic personages, assets, and locations and this book.

The publisher, author, and this book express no opinion on any actual historical incidences or actual historical persons referenced in this book.

**Like this book?**

If you like this author's work, your favorable review would be greatly appreciated at https://www.amazon.com/review/create-review?&asin=B0CZZ8JG21

**Other publications by this author may be found at:**

http://www.priatipub.com

*Languages of the World – A Multi-Lingual Introduction to Letters from Around the Globe – Volume 1* ***[2017 eLit Gold Award for Education / Academics / Teaching]***

*Languages of the World – A Multi-Lingual Introduction to Numbers from Around the Globe – Volume 2* ***[2017 eLit Gold Award for Children's Books (7 & Under)]***

*Languages of the World – A Multi-Lingual Introduction to Words from Around the Globe – Volume 3* ***[2018 eLit Gold Award for Education / Academics / Teaching]***

*The Rest Areas of Your Life* with Study Guide

*A Practical Approach to Parenting*

*Two Images of God* – (Suspense Novel Series)
   Book 1 – *Quest* ***[2018 Reader's Favorite Finalist]***
   Book 2 – *Discontent*
   Book 3 – *Conflict*
   Book 4 - *Resolution*

## Dedication

For our kids, in hopes they and their children will live in a world in which peace overshadows violence.

To my wife, who dedicated countless hours reviewing manuscripts, edits, and providing valuable feedback to improve the quality of the story.

For all people everywhere, regardless of their religion, ethnicity, or geographic location - that they may learn to listen to one another, accept our collective differences, and remember that we all inhabit the same planet as one people – as humanity, in a vast universe in which there is no dawning and no sunset.

## Preface

This book series is an illustration of the futility of protracted conflict based upon religious ideology. It shows how those with malice in their hearts can come from any religion or political group and negatively impact those in this world who prefer peace.

*Quest* (Book 1) explored how people of varying religious backgrounds can live and work together in peace.

*Discontent* (Book 2) explored the other side of the issue, involving those who would desire to wage war over those who would seek peace.

*Conflict* (Book 3) details how the darker side of human existence yields death and destruction, rather than achieving the dreams of those involved.

*Resolution* (Book 4) closes out our story by contrasting the losses associated with the worst of human nature with the benefits reflected in how our global society can achieve greatness when pulling together as a common people. It also reveals that a final solution may require both an innovative approach and a departure from historical precedence.

As was previously stated in *Quest*, "conflicts can be avoided. Human nature makes it a challenge."

This book series poses the question: Why can't we all get along?

Notes to the Reader

There are a few notes worth mentioning that will increase your enjoyment of this fictional work.

1. Character Names
   Continuing the name methodology from the previous books in this series, this book uses only the character's primary name to ease remembering their role in the story.

2. Time Indicator
   As with previous books in this series, this book takes the reader on a journey through a period of time. The author continues to make use of old-styled missile launch verbiage (i.e. "T plus"). For usage in this book, it has been shortened this to read "T+".

3. In this series, Book 3 (*Two Images of God-Conflict)* and Book 4 *(Two Images of God – Resolution)* are continuations of the parallel storylines developed in Book 1 (*Two Images of God-Quest)* and Book 2 (*Two Images of God-Discontent)*. A greater understanding the story will be revealed if the books are read in sequence.

4. General Information
   Any cited information is included in End Notes.

# Table of Contents

# T+1 Hour

## 1H.1 Israeli Knesset

\* \* \* \* \* \* \* \* \* \* \* \* \* \* \* \* \* \* \* \* \* \* \* \* \* \*

It was 1:00pm.

The Israeli Prime Minister and the Knesset were holding a regularly scheduled legislative session in Givat Ram, Western Jerusalem. Unlike the legislative bodies of the British Parliament or the U.S. Congress, the Knesset was a unicameral legislature consisting of only one chamber or house.[1]

"It is a great day for the State of Israel!" began the Prime Minister. "I have received word from Arthur that *IWO* has favorably received the Western Alliance's counter-proposal regarding the reallocation of land in the Middle East."

The assembly of legislators responded in light applause, not fully understanding the meaning of his statement.

"What this will mean for our Jewish nation is the following:

One - Arab Muslims, formerly living in Israel, will confine their culture to a new country.

Two - this new country will be recognized by the United Nations for the purpose of international trade.

Three - there will be UN monitoring to ensure that there are no human rights violations, that there are no terrorist training camps, and no armed forces that could be used to threaten Israel.

And four, perhaps the most important provision for our country - the country of Israel reverts to an undivided country. This means the West Bank and the Gaza Strip revert to Israeli ownership. The Palestinians are going to relocate to the new Islamic country."

With this last pronouncement, all of the legislators rose to their feet with resounding applause and shouts of joy. For several minutes, there was near pandemonium as the impact of this new potential treaty was beginning to be understood.

As the Prime Minister raised his hands for quiet, one of the Knesset members spoke up. "Does this mean that the Temple Mount will be returned to Israel? Can we now begin plans on reconstructing Solomon's Temple?"

The cacophony began to rise once again as the Prime Minister again motioned for quiet.

"My friends" he continued, "let's not get ahead of ourselves. While there is much yet to be accomplished, it would appear that one of our long-awaited dreams of an undivided country may be coming to realization. Once achieved, I personally feel that it is only a matter of time before it will be recognized by the world that the Temple Mount belongs to us.

Let us consider that Muslims already have three primary holy sites: the Masjid al-Haram Mosque in the city of Mecca; the Al-Masjid an-Nabawi Mosque in Medina; and the al-Ḥaram ash-Sharīf holy site here in Jerusalem. We, on the other hand, have no holy site or structure; rather, we are limited to the Western Wall, a mere fraction of what should be our holy site.

This great injustice will become clearer when the new Islamic country is formed. With the relocation of Arab Muslims from the new Israel, there will no longer be justification for them to have a holy site in the middle of our country, just as we would not demand a holy site in the middle of their new country. It is at that time, we will assert our right of eminent domain and reclaim the Temple Mount! It is at that time, we will begin rebuilding Solomon's Temple and fulfill our long-awaited destiny!"

The entire Knesset exploded in an uproar of jubilation at the thought of replacing Solomon's temple destroyed in 422 BCE and the Second Temple that was destroyed in 70 CE.

But the importance of this event held an even greater meaning for Jews. Because the building of this 'Third Temple' signaled the coming of the Messianic Age, an era of peace foretold by the Jewish prophet Isaiah in approximately 690 BCE . . . nearly 2,700 years ago!

Israel's long wait was finally coming to an end!

Or, so they thought.

A messenger entered the Knesset chamber and frantically hurried toward the Prime Minister who was standing by the lectern.

1H.2 Dig Site Aftermath

\* \* \* \* \* \* \* \* \* \* \* \* \* \* \* \* \* \* \* \* \* \* \* \* \* \* \*

In less than one hour, the dig site at the location of the ancient town of Dor, near present-day Nahsholim along the Mediterranean Coast, had been transformed into a war zone. Craters from exploded ordnance, destroyed vehicles, the wounded and dead littering the ground, all punctuated with the stains of blood on the sand of what earlier was a peaceful archaeology site.

A make-shift aid station had been set up in the southwest corner of the dig site behind the safety of armored vehicles. Ghaus and Sadia steadily tended to the wounded, whose medical severity had been previously determined by Esther to ensure those most in need were first tended. Army medics were handling the less severe cases to leverage the efforts of all available medical personnel. Talibah and Aaqil assisted by procuring needed medical supplies or holding bottles of plasma and saline solutions.

In less than forty-five minutes, forty-three casualties had occurred. Thirty-six were wounded while blankets covered the seven soldiers who had succumbed to their wounds.

Having been knocked unconscious by an RPG explosion, Moriah was beginning to awaken, complaining of head and ear pain. "I think you'll be alright" Esther said in reassurance. "You may have suffered a slight concussion from the blast and the ear pain is probably associated with the noise from the explosion. Just the same, we are sending you to the hospital for examination."

Moriah, now fully conscious, just nodded in compliance. She was still disoriented and not feeling up to conversation.

Jase took a bullet to the left shoulder, but it exited out his back leaving an unusually clean wound. The bullet did not hit any vital blood vessels or bone and, other than some blood loss and pain, he was ambulatory.

"You know," Sadia began, "you don't have to get shot to impress me. I am perfectly happy with the mild-mannered doctor that you were back at the hotel." She smiled at Jase and gave him a wink to help divert his attention away from his pain.

Trying to muster up as much machismo as he could, Jase replied "I thought you women always went for the 'hero' types" as he attempted a smile.

Resuming her role as a 'take charge' trauma nurse, Sadia replied "I am placing you on one of the medivacs. Just be sure you don't try to tell the surgeons at the hospital how to do their job! Just be a 'good' patient!" She signaled for one of the army medics to escort Jase to one of the waiting helicopters as she moved on to another patient.

Agnes was holding Frank's limp hand as he remained unconscious from his gunshot wound. Ghaus' trauma skills were serving him well as he treated the destruction to Frank's body. The terrorist's bullet had pierced his back, destroying his right lung prior to exiting his chest. Unlike Jase who had a "clean" wound, Frank was having difficulty breathing as well as suffering from massive blood loss due to the bullet having severed his pulmonary artery.

When medical personnel were not attending any specific patients, the four University of Jordan coeds circulated among the wounded, holding the patient's hand and offering words of comfort. Michael, Agnes, Abdul, and Hadiya softly spoke prayers of reassurance to the wounded Israeli soldiers and dig personnel. Sophie was hand-escorted by Michael to keep her from becoming overwrought by Frank's medical condition.

Sunni, Shia, Catholic, Hebrew, Arab, and Protestant – their cultural and theological identity no longer mattered. There were only those in need and those who provided comfort.

Within an hour following the attack, Israeli medivac helicopters began arriving at the ancient Dor dig site to transport the wounded to the Rambam Health Care Campus, located eight miles to the north in Haifa. Just outside the dust cloud created by the helicopter rotors, a lone V-22 Osprey aircraft landed to remove the seven dead soldiers, draped under blankets, to the regional army barracks located in Tel Aviv, one hundred miles to the south.

And, in the middle of the commotion, stood Colonel Beagan, a rifle in one hand and a radio in the other. This attack was more than just an assault on an archaeology dig site. It was an attack on his homeland. The resolute expression on his face, as he issued orders to the troops, revealed that, to him, this attack was personal.

1H.3 Arthur's Escape

\* \* \* \* \* \* \* \* \* \* \* \* \* \* \* \* \* \* \* \* \* \* \* \* \* \* \*

Arthur's Challenger 650 was running low on fuel. The aerial dogfight with the Navy Hornets, while lasting long enough to be convincing, had dipped into the fuel reserves his pilot had been relying on.

"We're going to need to find a gas station soon" Jefferson yelled out. Arthur came up to the cockpit and replied "Where are we now?"

The co-pilot pointed to a position on the map approximately halfway between the U.S. border and the tip of Baja California Sur. "Sir, it shows a small airstrip located just north of the coastal town of Bahia de los Angeles, located along the eastern shore of the Baja California Peninsula . . . about fifteen minutes flying time."

"There's our gas station. How large is the runway?" inquired Jefferson.

The co-pilot softly whistled as he located the airport information on his digital equipment. "It's only 5,000 feet long and this Challenger requires 5,500 feet. It looks like it's going to be too short."

Jefferson turned and winked at Arthur. "Up for another adventure?"

By now, Arthur had become accustomed to Jefferson's daring flying tendencies and knew from the wink that they would be landing on a very short runway in Bahia de los Angeles.

After ten more minutes, they passed through the last valley leading to the Gulf of California. Immediately in front of their aircraft was the airfield located by the co-pilot.

Jefferson banked the aircraft to the north with the intent of flying a right-downwind pattern to Runway 17. Deploying the landing gear and full flaps to slow the aircraft as much as possible, Jefferson banked slowly to the right as he descended in altitude to line up with the runway.

Suddenly, the aircraft shuttered, accompanied by a popping sound. Just as the aircraft began yawing to the right, Jefferson applied left rudder and aileron to control the aircraft's direction. "Sounds like we just lost the starboard engine!" he shouted. "Fuel selector to port!"

As the co-pilot responded to the emergency, he began calling out speed, altitude, and distance to the runway.

Jefferson turned toward Arthur. "This has turned out to be interesting, don't you think?"

Standing in the doorway leading to the cockpit, Arthur repeatedly exchanged his glances between the view out of the windscreen and Jefferson's apparent calm at losing an engine due to fuel shortage.

The aircraft was now only feet above the sandy desert when the sudden squeal of tires on asphalt resounded through the cabin. Jefferson had managed to land within the first ten feet of the runway and was now applying all of the braking and reverse thrust he could to stop the aircraft. Seconds seemed like minutes, but the aircraft came to a standstill with five hundred feet of runway remaining.

The look on the co-pilot's face was priceless. "Sir, you shouldn't have been able to do that! The aircraft manual said 'a minimum of 5,500 feet' and you only used 4,500 feet of runway!"

Jefferson realized he had been extremely lucky but disguised his relief to ensure his pilot bravado remained intact. "All in a day's work" he casually replied.

"Kudos to your piloting skills" offered Arthur. "But, how are you in locating some fuel?"

"Not a problem" replied Jefferson. "I used to fly down here from the states whenever I was on vacation. Let me make some phone calls. I'm sure we can have JET A-1 fuel within a couple of hours. "Don't take too long" Arthur cautioned. "I'm sure they are looking for us" pointing upward as a reference to the spy satellite that had been obviously used to track their earlier movement.

As Jefferson pulled the jet under an open-air shelter to hide the aircraft from surveillance satellites, Arthur returned to his seat in the cabin to ponder his next move. He had to figure out a way to wrest control of Western Alliance forces away from

Clancy to avoid the very conflict he and Abbas were working to prevent.

1H.4 Abbas' Escape

* * * * * * * * * * * * * * * * * * * * * * * * * *

Clancy could not believe his luck. In the span of twenty-four hours, his intelligence unit had received information on the locations of three of *IWO's* top leaders – Abbas, Fathi, and Sayyid. With that information, he had his operations unit develop plans for drone attacks on each of the targets, taking advantage of his global distribution of Western Alliance forces.

But, the real prize was Abbas. The idea of taking out *IWO's* leader and master strategist was just too enticing. Besides, with his failed attempt to get rid of Arthur, Clancy needed a big win to reinforce his move to wrest control of the Western Alliance away from Arthur, Kruglov, and Pao.

He followed the progress of the Predator drones via satellite imagery as they silently flew to their targets. But with Abbas, Clancy decided to also mobilize a sniper team to ensure 'the kill' took place.

* * * * * * * * * * * * * * * * * * * * * * * * * *

Abbas had been a warrior too long to not listen to his gut feeling that something was amiss. Just prior to the missile strike from the MQ-1 Predator drone, Abbas had moved into the café and made his way to the back of the building. Seconds later, three Griffin rockets struck the front of the café where he had been sitting.

The concussion of the blast had thrown him out the back door of the café, thus protecting him from the explosions. However, those out front and in the street were not so lucky.

Young, old, male, female – all were cast into the air like rag dolls as the shock wave dissipated outward from the blast zone. Those not killed outright by the blast wave from the explosions were shredded by the shards of glass from nearby stores. Still others were cut down by chucks of concrete.

Those not injured by the blast revealed facial expressions of horror and shock, their minds not able to grasp the magnitude of the devastation or the immediacy of its impact. Some froze in place, appearing like store mannequins, not sure if they should move to safety or remain in place for safety. Then silence.

Utter silence.

\* \* \* \* \* \* \* \* \* \* \* \* \* \* \* \* \* \* \* \* \* \* \* \* \*

The sniper team took their cue from the explosions. As the dust began to settle from the explosions, they began to see movement among the local population who were searching for survivors.

But, Clancy had been very clear – Abbas was not to survive this attack. Unfortunately, at their distance of 1,000 meters, they could not discern facial features with sufficient clarity to confirm if they were shooting at the right target. So, the expedient approach was to shoot anyone resembling Abbas.

The two shooters took aim at any male who had attire similar to what Abbas had been wearing.

Shots rang out.

After ten Arab men had been shot, other men in the village realized that movement in the open would result in more casualties. To avoid detection, people either remained indoors or lay motionless in the street.

In the meantime, Abbas tried to gather his thoughts as he lay in the sand outside the back of the café ruins. As he began to wonder how someone could have known his location so precisely, he began hearing distant gunfire. But, it was not the noise associated with ordinary assault weapons.

Those were sniper rifles. Someone was going to extreme lengths to ensure he would be killed.

Had he misread Arthur in spite of all the discussions they had during those previous meetings? Was this Aarzam beginning to make a move to wrest leadership of *IWO* from him? Or, maybe it was Fathi or Sayyid making their move to assume control?

Whoever it was, he had to move quickly to determine the state of affairs within *IWO*'s leadership and his relationship with Arthur.

Using the buildings to conceal his movement, he rose to his feet and stumbled toward a small pickup truck.

## 1H.5 Arab Discussion of New Islamic State

\* \* \* \* \* \* \* \* \* \* \* \* \* \* \* \* \* \* \* \* \* \* \* \* \* \* \*

Following the *IWO* concession discussions at NONRAD's Cheyenne Mountain Complex, leaders of the affected Arab countries had arranged to meet at the International Palace Hotel in Abu Dhabi, United Arab Emirates.

Now gathered in the Grand Auditorium were representatives from Yemen, Oman, the United Arab Emirates (UAE), Saudi Arabia, Iraq, Lebanon, Syria, Iran, Turkmenistan, Uzbekistan, Tajikistan, Afghanistan, and Pakistan.

As host of the event, the UAE Emir Al Qataum took his position at the podium with a map of the region appearing on a projector screen behind him.

"Gentlemen, let me refresh our collective memories regarding the *IWO* proposal that has been submitted for our review.

One, the majority of United Nations (UN) countries have agreed to the formation of a new Islamic state or country for Arab Muslims now living in Israel.

Two, this new country will receive official recognition by the UN.

Three, it was proposed that a consortium of Arab countries provide financial and construction support to create the needed infrastructure.

Four, the UN also agreed there would be no outside interference, with two notable exceptions. First, this new country must comply with UN mandates on human rights. In addition, auditors will be dispatched to ensure that the harshest aspects of our religion are not unleashed on our citizenry. This would include aspects of the Qur'an, the Sunnah, the Hadith, and any other documents governing Muslim life. This would include, but not be limited to, female sexual mutilation, a presumption of female guilt in cases of rape, honor beatings and killings, and the right for women to pursue education. In addition, there must be no terrorist training camps or indoctrination centers designed to recruit and train terrorists.

It should be noted that Jordan has elected not to be a part of this new Islamic country.

Finally, the country of Israel reverts to an undivided country. That means the West Bank and the Gaza Strip revert to Israeli ownership. Thus, all Palestinians will relocate to the new Islamic country.

Are there any questions before we start?"

The Iranian president rose to his feet. "Who will run this new country? Will it be Sunni or Shia?" At once, voices of argument began to rise to a crescendo.

The Emir knew he had to regain control of the discussion. "Gentlemen, gentlemen" as he raised his arms to calm the attendees. "We have many, many items that need to be discussed over the next few days. The political structure of this new Islamic country is only one of many topics. Let's maintain a level of decorum that will lead to the resolution of those issues."

The King of Saudi Arabia rose to his feet. "Emir, I applaud your efforts to lead us in these discussions. However, I believe that it will take more than a few days to resolve all of the related issues. There are even some for which we will need to negotiate with Israel, such as access to our holy site of al-Ḥaram ash-Sharīf in Jerusalem. How will that occur?"

Retaining his position at the lectern, the Emir continued.

"I am aware of the magnitude of these discussions. My desire is that we establish two goals for this meeting. One, that we lay out the specific issues related to each of the five provisions of this proposal. And two, that we define a framework for how to resolve each one in the future.

This proposal has the potential of achieving great things for the Islamic people. But, with global tensions being so high, I fear that our time for resolving these issues is limited. The sooner we can come to an understanding, the greater the probability of deescalating the brewing global conflict."

The Emir was about to introduce an idea for framing the discussions when an aide entered the auditorium and quickly made his way up to the stage. As the aide began speaking quietly, the smile on the Emir's face disappeared.

## 1H.6 Knesset Response

\* \* \* \* \* \* \* \* \* \* \* \* \* \* \* \* \* \* \* \* \* \* \* \* \* \* \*

The news of the terrorist attack on the Dor archaeology dig site near Nahsholim took the Prime Minister by surprise. He was torn between taking an immediate military response against known terrorist organizations and taking the time to address members of the Knesset who would want to 'discuss' military options. He opted for an abbreviated acknowledgement to the latter in favor of having tactical discussions with his military chiefs within the hour.

"Gentlemen" he began. "I have just received news that the international dig site near Nahsholim has just been attacked by terrorist forces. There were forty-three casualties, seven of which were our brave soldiers who gave their lives for Israel."

The Knesset grew eerily quiet as members processed the news.

The Prime Minister continued. "Although our forces defeated the terrorists, there was substantive damage to the dig site. The Directors of the IMA and EMA are in transit to our location to provide more information about the personnel and to discuss the status of the dig."

One member rose to his feet. "We cannot let terrorists dictate how we run our country or efforts aimed at uncovering the history of our country! While the military is pursuing the responsible terrorist organizations, we should also double our efforts to re-open the dig site as quickly as possible. It is important for the world to see that we are not intimidated by criminal acts!"

Shouts of support echoed across the chamber as opposing political factions became united under these common causes – the eradication of terrorism and the preservation of the Jewish state.

1H.7 Arab Response to Dig Site Attack

\* \* \* \* \* \* \* \* \* \* \* \* \* \* \* \* \* \* \* \* \* \* \* \* \* \* \* \*

Following the impromptu briefing by his aid, UAE Emir Al Qataum returned to his position at the podium, his face reflecting a note of concern.  He held up his hands to signify quiet within the Grand Ballroom of the International Palace Hotel in Abu Dhabi, United Arab Emirates.

"My friends" he began.  "I have just received word that the Arab-Israeli joint archaeology dig taking place at the location of the ancient town of Dor, near present-day Nahsholim, Israel was attacked by a terrorist group less than twelve hours ago.  There have been multiple casualties, including Israeli soldiers and civilian dig personnel.  The terrorist forces were killed by the Israeli military but their identity has yet to be confirmed.

My friends, this attack has the potential of causing great harm to the progress for peace with the Western Alliance, including the creation of the new Islamic State."

As the Emir was concluding his remarks, cell phones began ringing among members of the audience.  One by one, they began hearing about Clancy's drone attack against the village of Harjiwan.

The Iranian president again rose to his feet and began striding toward the podium at the front of the room, his right hand thrusted into the air with his cellphone. "You speak of peace while the infidels from the Western Alliance are bombing our land! Look at the video coming in from the village of Harjiwan! Look at all of our dead brothers and sisters in the street! Look at all of the dead children!"

When he got to the stage, he synchronized his phone to the laptop powering the video presentation. Soon, the video from his phone was being shown to everyone in the ballroom on a twelve-foot-wide projection screen. The raw cell phone footage revealed the devastation of the drone strike, the collapsed buildings, and the bodies of the dead lying in the village square. Haze from the blasts clouded the video images, making it appear that the attack was recent.

The Iranian president continued. "This is the treachery of the West! This is how they are two-faced, speaking of peace while, at the same time, sending their drones to attack and kill fellow our fellow Arabs! They are seeking to destroy the Arab culture by systematically exterminating our people!

Well, two can play that game! Iran is now a nuclear country and we will unleash are arsenal against the west with devastating fury!"

The room erupted in angry shouts, some joining the Iranian president in declaring all-out war against the West while others opposed the use of violence to retain hope in the formation of an Islamic State.

The UAE Emir knew it was imperative that he regain control of the delegates until the nature of the attacks on the archaeology site and the village of Harjiwan could be determined.

Taking the microphone from the Iranian president, the Emir once again addressed the audience. Although it took several minutes of gesturing and words of calm, the room began to quiet as audience members took their seats.

"This news is disturbing" he began. "But what we don't know at this time is whether the West's attack on Harjiwan had anything to do with the terrorist attack on the Arab-Israeli archaeology site. We cannot succumb to emotion until all of the facts are known. I urge you all to maintain your composure. Abbas has worked long and hard to place us in a position to effectively negotiate with the West on the formation of a new Islamic State. Let us not throw away all his hard work based on supposition and incomplete information."

The Iranian president stormed off the stage and left the room. While some in the audience thought of following him, they remained seated, convinced by the Emir's argument to give peace a chance.

Little did he know more attacks would come that would threaten the tender support for peace he had created in that room.

# T+1 Day

## 1D.1 Frank's Demise

\* \* \* \* \* \* \* \* \* \* \* \* \* \* \* \* \* \* \* \* \* \* \* \* \* \*

It was late in the afternoon before the rest of the dig team could travel to the hospital to check on the condition of those that were injured in the attack.

Moriah seemed to be okay but was being held overnight due to her concussion from the blast. Jase, his arm bandaged and in a sling, was walking from room to room checking on those soldiers who had been wounded defending the dig site. While he could not render medical attention due to his injury, his experience as a trauma surgeon dealing with combat wounds made him useful to the medical staff.

Ghaus, Sadia, and Hadiya were quickly moving from bed to bed in the recovery ward, ensuring those coming out of surgery were in stable condition.

Michael, Agnes, Abdul, and Hadiya also visited the wounded in each of their rooms to provide the kind of compassion that only a person of clergy could offer. The labels of Christian, Muslim, and Hebrew continued to hold no significance as those who were in need appreciated those who were there to serve.

Sophie was pacing the length of the hallway, worried about Frank who remained in surgery. Aaqil and Talibah walked with her, providing what comfort they could. Given their affection for each other, they understood the depth of Sophie's relationship with Frank and her concern for his welfare.

They had just made their countless laps of the hallway when the doors of the surgical suite swung open. Sophie's facial expression turned to one of hope as she expected to see Frank's gurney wheel through the doors and into the recovery ward. But the gurney never came. Instead, the lead surgeon came into the hallway and headed toward the IMA Director.

While it seemed to Sophie to take forever, she covered the length of the hallway in a matter of seconds to arrive beside the two men. They both turned toward her with expressions of sadness and outstretched arms of consolation. Embracing her softly, their silence told the story.

Frank was dead.

Sophie sank to the floor, sobbing uncontrollably just as Agnes emerged from one the patients' rooms. Immediately sensing the same emotion she felt following Michael's heart attack, she moved swiftly toward Sophie, sitting next to her on the floor and wrapped her motherly arms around her. Sophie was now a child needing comfort from one of life's harsh realities.

A few minutes later, Abdul emerged from a patient's room into the hallway. Seeing Agnes on the floor cradling Sophie told the story. Tears came to his eyes as he moved toward them, lending emotional support to a Westerner in need.

## 1D.2 Aarzam's Response to Abbas Drone Attack

\* \* \* \* \* \* \* \* \* \* \* \* \* \* \* \* \* \* \* \* \* \* \* \* \* \*

Aarzam stood in front of his office window, slowly stroking his beard, contemplating his imminent rise to be the new leader of *IWO*. His well-crafted assassination plots against Abbas, Sayyid, and Fathi were nearing completion, thus eliminating any competition to his rise to dominance.

The sudden ringing of his telephone interrupted his thoughts. On the other end of the phone was his head of *IWO's* covert agents.

"We have just received word that the American drone attack has occurred. Four missiles strikes were observed at the north end of Harjiwan that obliterated numerous buildings, including the café. We are awaiting confirmation of Abbas' death."

"That's great news!" exclaimed Aarzam. "Be sure to let me know as soon as we have any word about the strikes on Sayyid and Fathi."

"Will do" was the brief reply on the other end as the covert agent hung up the phone.

As he slowly rubbed his chin, Aarzam mused *'One down . . . two more to go'*.

## 1D.3 Target:  Fathi

\* \* \* \* \* \* \* \* \* \* \* \* \* \* \* \* \* \* \* \* \* \* \* \* \* \* \*

Two days ago, Aarzam had called Fathi with intelligence data regarding an incursion by a Western Alliance Special Forces unit to the border between Sa'dah, Yemen and Najran, Saudi Arabia.  Incensed at the idea that the West would be so bold as to launch a strike in his territory, Fathi had taken a dozen of his best fighters to his secret outpost located in Hangar 7 at the airport west of Sa'dah.

Arriving at the airfield near midnight, his men entered the hangar and began organizing the weapons previously secured from the storage lockers.  Soon, the hangar floor began to resemble a combat staging area with neatly arranged rows of AK-47 rifles, hand grenades, night-vision goggles, and ammunition bandoleers.

By 2:00am, preparations were complete.  This gave Fathi and his team a day to rest prior to a nighttime raid on the Western Special Forces unit.

As he reclined on his cot, Fathi began to fantasize about his rise to *IWO* leadership.  *'I'll get rid of these Western infidels tomorrow night and then sweep IWO clean of Aarzam, Sayyid, and Abbas.  Once they're out of the way, then my rise to control all of IWO will be complete.'*

He began to doze off just as the first Griffin rocket fired from a MQ-1 Predator drone aircraft rocketed through the hangar window.

The efficiency at which Aarzam's covert agents were able to engage known double-agents for the Western Alliance was just short of amazing. Within twenty-four hours, they had been able to disclose the GPS coordinates of Fathi's secret outpost and the date and time he would be at that location.

Within a few hours, that information had filtered up through the Western Alliance intelligence network and had been verified. It only took minutes to provide the information to the Predator Drone Command Center for targeting. Given the proximity of the target to Western Alliance forces, the mission was given a high priority.

Since the Predator arrived at the target location a few hours before Fathi's arrival, the drone pilot and weapons officer were able to track Fathi's movements as they entered the hangar. Allowing sufficient time to what they guessed would be the arrangement of weapons and explosives for an *IWO* assault on the Western Alliance position, the drone operators launched three missiles in three second intervals, leaving one missile in reserve in the event anyone emerged from the destroyed hangar.

The Predator remained on site for another fifteen minutes following the third missile strike. After no one emerged from the demolished building, the drone operators decided to launch a fourth missile for good measure just as rescue personnel were arriving on scene to investigate the series of explosions.

There were no survivors.

## 1D.4 Target: Kruglov

\* \* \* \* \* \* \* \* \* \* \* \* \* \* \* \* \* \* \* \* \* \* \* \* \* \*

While Sayyid was proceeding to the Port of Sohar, his IRGC forces located at Khvoy, Iran had been assessing information obtained from double agents in the West regarding the location of Kruglov.

The message they received indicated that Kruglov had arrived two days ago at a small airbase located just southeast of the Tbilisi International Airport in Tbilisi, Georgia. He was establishing a field headquarters in a series of buildings just east of the runway.

With IRGC forces located at Khvoy Iran, only 230 air miles to the south, Tbilisi's close proximity would permit Sayyid to launch an air strike to take out one of the Western Alliance's top generals.

However, it did not go without notice to Sayyid that he was the unusual beneficial recipient of three extraordinary pieces of intelligence information – one regarding the Western Alliance general staff location in the Port of Sohar; the second being the field headquarters location for Kruglov; and the third being the field headquarters location for Pao.

The information seemed to have come too easy. The first was a 'gift' from Aarzam and the second was through a network of double agents. It was all too easy.

Sayyid began to wonder if there were mutinous factions within the Western Alliance that were seeking its demise. Had Arthur, Pao, and Kruglov lost their influence? Were political pressures mounting to cause friction between the countries making up the Alliance?

Sayyid continued to wonder as he spoke with his operations officer at the IRGC airbase in Khvoy. The officer began his telephone briefing to Sayyid.

"At a target range of only 230 miles, we should be able to launch, execute the strike, and return from the mission within 72 minutes at an airspeed of 400 knots. The aircraft will be flying low level, nap-of-the-earth to avoid radar detection. The mission should only require one pass with four aircraft - two will target the command building and two will target the adjacent hangars. Each Sukhoi Su-24 aircraft will carry two 1,000-pound bombs to ensure total annihilation of the targets. The aircraft and pilots are ready for your orders."

Sayyid thought for a moment. '*This just seems too easy*' he thought. "Very well. Launch the attack at dusk so the setting sun will mask our incoming aircraft. Make sure the pilots know the Russians use listening posts for below-radar surveillance, so they should fly accordingly to keep their noise signature to a minimum."

"Yes sir!" was the prompt reply.

* * * * * * * * * * * * * * * * * * * * * * * * *

Meanwhile, as Kruglov moved around within the remote headquarters at Tbilisi, he sighed at the absence of the refinements of the luxurious Moscow accommodations to which he was accustomed. While his staff had ensured his Tbilisi headquarters was far more pleasant than any other field headquarters in the Russian military, he still missed his pampered existence. But, the presence of Tanya, his favorite escort, seemed to lessen the dreariness of this remote location.

His team had spent the last couple of days placing the outdated, Cold War communications equipment in working order. Since Pao and he had experienced issues with non-loyal staff, both had decided to operate from remote locations for secrecy and security. As for Arthur, he had avoided being shot down by his own Western Alliance aircraft and was now somewhere in Baja California.

As dusk settled over the airfield, Kruglov announced to his staff that he would be taking his dinner in the bomb shelter several stories below the main floor of the headquarters building. It was not out of fear but in deference to the privacy he desired to have with Tanya.

As the elevator doors closed behind them, several of the staff shook their heads and smiled, wishing they were of a rank and position that would afford them the same level of "pleasure" in their own military lives.

Kruglov and Tanya had just seated themselves for dinner when time seemed to stop. Three stories above, each member of Kruglov's staff disintegrated into thin air as the first two Iranian bombs exploded in rapid succession, leveling the building. The next two explosions occurred fifteen seconds later as the second Iranian aircraft targeting the command headquarters released its ordnance. What were chunks of concrete left over from the first blast turned to dust at the detonation of the second set of 1,000-pound bombs.

The adjacent hangar underwent a similar air strike, two aircraft attacking in sequence. However, with the aircraft parked inside the hangars, combined with nearby fuel storage tanks, the magnitude of the resulting detonations lit up the darkening sky. Windows in the Tbilisi Airport terminal two miles away shattered at the force of the nearby explosions, with portions of the ceiling structure caving in on passengers awaiting flights.

Forty feet below the surface, Kruglov had just sat down to his evening meal with Tanya when he heard two muffled booms in close succession. As he paused pouring the red wine he so highly favored, a second set of muffled booms rattled the dinnerware.

"What's going on?" Tanya asked, a look of concern replacing her previous smile.

Kruglov had been a soldier too long to mistake the sound of heavy ordnance finding its mark. He put the wine bottle down, wondering if anyone above had been able to survive.

Entombed forty feet below the surface, he also wondered how he would get out. Through the elevator's glass panel, he could see the shaft filling with debris and dust seeping through the bottom of the elevator doors.

His mind was racing as he returned Tanya's questioning expression with a blank stare.

1D.5 Target:  Pao #1

\* \* \* \* \* \* \* \* \* \* \* \* \* \* \* \* \* \* \* \* \* \* \* \* \* \*

It was long rumored that the Pakistan Army's Special Services Group (SSG)[2] had an under-the-table relationship with Iran's IRGC.  Initially formed to mirror the capabilities of the U.S. Special Forces, SSG's 5600-man force focused on counter-terrorism activities.  But, like many military organizations, there were some SSG leaders who had other agendas and Sayyid was an expert at ferreting out this information to his advantage.

Starting nearly a decade ago, Sayyid began courting influential members of the Pakistani military to develop mutually beneficial 'economic opportunities'.  This was quite a challenge given that Pakistan was primarily Sunni while Iran was primarily Shia.  Little did he know at the time that he was playing into the future strategic plans of Abbas and the formation of *IWO*.

Combining their efforts with closely aligned members of Pakistani intelligence, a small faction of the SSG began a secret relationship with Sayyid's IRGC, participating in joint operations that would mutually benefit the geopolitical spheres of influence desired by each group.  Now, they worked together in a small, nondescript building on the outskirts of Islamabad.

It was at this consolidated forces facility that Clancy's message regarding the location of Pao was received from a double agent.

*"See attached satellite photo.  Pao is located near the Hotan Airport in China.  He has three*

> *command and control buildings on the south end*
> *of the airfield adjacent to two private hangars.*
> *Pao and his general staff should be there for*
> *another five days. After that, their whereabouts*
> *will be unknown."*

Given Sayyid's role in *IWO* and his known interest in keeping track of Western Alliance leaders, the Islamabad team wasted no time in contacting him for guidance on this latest intelligence.

Sayyid was aboard the Qahr when the radio transmission came through from the joint operations facility in Islamabad.

His IRGC coordinator began "Sayyid, we just received word through our intelligence courier network regarding Pao. The information was obtained from our Western Alliance contacts and discusses Pao's location at a remote base in China. It intimates that the location may be ripe for a strike during the next two days."

Sayyid was both interested and duly cautious. "Why would the West 'leak' such information about one their leaders? That doesn't make any sense."

"Well, maybe not" the officer continued "but, Pao represents both one of the top three military leaders for the West as well as head of one the largest armies in the world that could pose a threat to *IWO*. Removing him would aid our cause."

Sayyid had to silently acknowledge his officer's last statement. *Removing Pao would be a great boon to IWO's*

*cause. But, this seemed too easy; the information too precise.*
*Was this intelligence fortuitous or was it a trap?*

"Sir, what would you like us to do? Pao's location in Hotan
China is approximately 430 air miles from Islamabad and only
one hundred miles from our eastern border. We could fly an air
sortie with fighter-bombers or parachute troops and vehicles near
the border for a ground assault. In any case, we will need to act
quickly since the information we received indicated that he will
only be in Hotan for two more days."

Sayyid responded to the young energetic voice on the other
end of the radio. "How do you know this isn't a trap? That the
information is valid? You could be sending our troops to their
deaths."

"But sir, this information came through our intelligence
network in the West. They have always been reliable before.
Besides, this is just too great an opportunity to pass up!"

Sayyid paused. While he knew he should devote more time
to this action, he was concentrating more on the recent mission
information from the air strike in Tbilisi and the upcoming
mission in the Port of Sohar. After a few moments, he relented.

"Okay" he responded. "Go ahead and strike the target. But,
the Chinese will have a significant number of troops on the
ground given Pao's presence, so a ground attack would be
unwise. Launch an air strike and remind the pilots to remain at
low altitude to avoid the radar that will be looking for them.
Keep me advised."

The young officer strained to moderate his excitement. "I'll take care of this for you, Sayyid. You can rest assured the mission will be successful. Pao is as good as dead."

Sayyid returned the microphone to his communications technician. As he turned to the ladder leading up to the *Qahr's* bridge, he wondered if he had treated this latest opportunity against the West too lightly. Was it a trap or was it a gift from Allah?

He would soon find out.

\* \* \* \* \* \* \* \* \* \* \* \* \* \* \* \* \* \* \* \* \* \* \* \*

Pao remained troubled by the lack of professionalism in his military organization disclosed less than one week ago. His subsequent interrogations and 'purge' of discredited personnel was an effective response to incentivize his remaining officers to be more diligent in their duties. Nonetheless, he was chagrined at having to admit his military's blunder to Arthur and Kruglov, something that violated the notion of 'saving face'.

It wasn't like him to ponder past actions. But, as he stood in his Hotan field office, looking out the window toward the mountains rising to the southwest, he wondered if that blunder by those under his command would negatively impact his continued rise in power.

The office was a hive of activity with old equipment being brought online and new equipment being installed. Partially obscured by the dust blowing across the arid landscape, troops were on the move outside, deliberate in their tasks to ready the command center and surrounding base for action. Fighter and transport aircraft were landing at the airfield to augment the base's military readiness.

Pao smiled, pleased with the efficiency with which his people were executing their duties. It probably helped that all were keenly aware of the 'purge' that had occurred over the last few days as a result of the weapons loss revealed by his staff officer Chin. He had found that it proved useful in the past to have 'purges' every so often – it kept everyone aware of their duties and increased unit efficiency.

However, it would not be until later that Pao would truly appreciate how this renewed troop effectiveness would become serendipitous.

1D.6 Target:  Sayyid

\* \* \* \* \* \* \* \* \* \* \* \* \* \* \* \* \* \* \* \* \* \* \* \* \* \*

It was night-time as the *Qahr*, Sayyid's high-tech command ship, gently pulled into the ship channel leading to the Port of Sohar.  Sayyid was following up on some intelligence received from Aarzam two days earlier that the Western Alliance was establishing a forward operating base in an abandoned warehouse at the Port of Sohar in Oman.  Given that it was to become the regional headquarters for West's Middle East general staffs, Sayyid had been convinced that it would be a great target of opportunity.

"Sayyid!" the helmsman exclaimed.  "Sonar is picking up two small boats" in the channel ahead of us."

Sayyid had just climbed the ladder leading from the ship's command center to the bridge, where he had been monitoring radio traffic relating to the building conflict between *IWO* and the Western Alliance.  "It's not unusual to find small boats out in the channel.  What has you worried?" Sayyid asked.

"I am worried because they haven't moved in the last thirty minutes" the helmsman responded.  "They're just sitting there, one on either side of the channel.  At this time of night, why aren't they headed to their berth in the harbor?"

Sayyid spotted the small boats on the *Qahr's* sonar screen. Looking up through the windscreen, he raised the binoculars to his eyes to peer into the distance, just as the two small craft were coming into view.  They were 31-foot sport yachts, positioned several hundred yards apart on either side of the channel. They were both maintaining a position that would allow them to head toward the middle of the channel.

*The yeoman was right,* Sayyid thought. *At this time of night, why would two sport yachts be sitting mid-channel?*

"All Stop" Sayyid ordered. Now a hundred meters closer, Sayyid could just make out the exhaust plumes on each boat, a tell-tale sign that that the engines on sport yachts were idling.

Sayyid couldn't place his finger on why 'alarms' were sounding in his head. But, he had learned long ago to trust his 'fight or flight' inclinations.

Turning toward his intelligence director, he barked "Get the assault team into their boats. We'll see if these two sport yachts become a problem.

Twelve of Sayyid's Quds commandos made their way into two motorized dinghies, small flexible-sided rafts with motors. Armed with automatic weapons and RPG's, they pushed away from the *Qahr* and began motoring quietly toward the Port of Sohar.

After the two dinghies had gone two hundred meters, Sayyid notices movement aboard the two mysterious yachts. Crewmen were now on deck, seemingly running in multiple directions. But what was most noticeable was that they were armed with assault rifles and pointing toward the Sayyid's small assault teams now passing their position.

The water suddenly churned at the sterns of both yachts as their engines came alive to full throttle, slowly gaining speed as they headed toward the two motorized dinghies heading into the Port.

Sayyid's intelligence director, now standing beside Sayyid on the bridge, lifted his handheld radio to his mouth. "You have enemies at your six-o'clock position and closing. Use your RPG's and return to the ship. We've been set up!" he shouted.

One member of the Quds commandos on each dinghy retrieved Russian-made RPG's, aimed carefully and fired, almost at the same time.

Aboard the yachts, Aarzam's men were confused. They had been under orders to destroy Sayyid's command ship. But, when it did not enter the harbor and, instead, launched two motorized dinghies, they were at a loss for direction. Eventually coming to the conclusion that Sayyid might be aboard one of the dinghies, they decided to give chase to kill everyone aboard the small craft.

They left their holding positions on either side of the of the channel entrance. As their speed increased and they got to within fifty meters of their prey, they noticed streaks of light coming at their yachts from the dinghies. Before they could react to the realization that RPG's had been fired at them, both yachts exploded, as the rocket propelled grenades found their respective marks.

With the secondary detonation of the ammunition aboard each yacht, the night sky lit up like day as the sound of the explosions reverberated across the harbor.

Not wanting his men to be challenged by harbor security forces, Sayyid gave the command to the helmsman to move the *Qahr* forward briskly to shorten the return distance and time for his commandos to re-board the *Qahr*. Ten minutes later, they were headed out of the Port of Sohar and into the safety of the open waters of the Gulf of Oman.

Sayyid now knew where Aarzam stood in his quest for control of *IWO*. As he considered the events that had just transpired, an 18th century proverb came to mind *'Revenge is a dish that is best served cold'*.

A smile crept to Sayyid's face as he thought of the pleasure he would receive when he exacted his revenge on Aarzam.

1D.7 First Cut

\* \* \* \* \* \* \* \* \* \* \* \* \* \* \* \* \* \* \* \* \* \* \* \* \* \*

The last twenty-four hours in Victoria Harbor reflected a scene of chaos. When the explosion of the ULCC oil tanker *Lockerman* occurred, the water of the harbor was awash in fire as the oil slick fed the inferno. The harbor master had frantically attempted to call for emergency response teams to mobilize; however, given the collateral damage throughout Hong Kong as a result of the explosion, he found himself competing with other city agencies trying to respond to their priorities.

Slowly, fire response boats appeared to deploy fire retardant on the oil that was ablaze on the water. Although damaged, other ships in the harbor had lowered tender boats to look for survivors in the water. Unfortunately for the crew of the *Lockerman*, their demise was a foregone conclusion. The force of the blast created a shockwave that was crushing in its effect.

In the intervening day, most of the fires had been extinguished, leaving only the burned remnants of the *Lockerman's* superstructure visible above the water. Oil booms and sorbents had been deployed to contain the oil slick while skimmers were being deployed to remove oil from the surface of the water.

Although the sinking of the *Lockerman* had made the global news networks within an hour of its occurrence, it was a singular event. No one initially thought to connect it to an act of terrorism. Aarzam had planned it this way. While his natural instinct was to hit the West in one large military action, he was beginning to appreciate the wisdom of the strategic thinking so often employed by Abbas.

Aarzam would defeat the West through 'death by a thousand cuts'. A practice thought to have originated in ancient China, *lingchi* was rumored to have been a form of execution in which the victim was slowly killed through series of non-fatal cuts.[3] It was the accumulation of the cuts that eventually killed the prisoner.

Applied to his war with the West, Aarzam's strategy was to slowly defeat his adversary through a series of events that, taken singularly, might amount to little. But, taken cumulatively, they would overpower the West's ability to respond effectively.

The *Lockerman* was the 'first cut'.

## 1D.8 Response to First Cut

\* \* \* \* \* \* \* \* \* \* \* \* \* \* \* \* \* \* \* \* \* \* \* \* \*

Clancy was nearly ecstatic. "I can't believe the luck we had in locating and taking out Abbas! What's the latest from our sniper team?"

Responding to Clancy's inquiry, Major Brannon, his intelligence staff officer, promptly entered Clancy's office to bring him up to date.

"The sniper team has reported that they have engaged ten hostiles from their position at a distance of 1,000 yards. Our over-watch drone is not reporting any unusual movement."

"Are they still in position?" barked Clancy.

"No" answered Brannon. "They remained at their position for fifteen minutes but had to withdraw when some villagers in an adjacent building heard their gunfire. Rather than risk another ground battle, they chose to egress the area for a helicopter pickup at their designated LZ."

Clancy rose from his chair and walked around to the front of his desk. "Let's go take a look at the drone footage."

Clancy was just exiting his office when his communications officer began running toward him from across the room.

Clancy paused, unaccustomed to such odd behavior from one of his officers in the headquarters building.

"Sir", the communications officer gasped. "You have to see this message!"

Clancy began reading the report on the *Lockerman,* the ULCC oil tanker which exploded in Hong Kong's Victoria Harbor on the prior day.

Somewhat exasperated, Clancy responded "I already know about the *Lockerman*! What's in here that's new?!"

"Read further . . . rescue teams found portions of the hull with indications that the explosions were caused by external detonations . . . the ship was purposely blown up!"

"Why should we care what goes on in Victoria Harbor" Clancy responded.

"Sir, look at where the ship was sunk? Not only did they damage other ships that were nearby with just one explosive event, the magnitude of the wreckage essentially blocks the entire shipping channel! The impact to global commerce at one of the busiest ports in the world has all the markings of *IWO*. Isn't this the kind of attack they would do?!"

Clancy paused to reflect on the young officer's observation. *Could IWO be launching a broad-based offensive initiative?* He rubbed his chin and slowly made his way over to the world map on the wall.

## 1D.9 Second Cut

\* \* \* \* \* \* \* \* \* \* \* \* \* \* \* \* \* \* \* \* \* \* \* \* \* \* \* \*

The *Norwegian Classic,* a 5,000-passenger luxury liner, was currently transiting the Atlantic Ocean on a 30-day world cruise. Coincidently following the same route the RMS Titanic took in April 1912, the large cruise ship was approaching the same geographic coordinates.

Passengers strolled along the decks while children enjoyed the outdoor entertainment on a warm afternoon. No one had a care in the world as the ship sliced through the water, dolphins leaping through the bow wave as the force of the ship propelled them forward. The ship's twenty-five knot speed provided a smooth ride for passengers as the ocean breeze blew across the decks.

On the bridge, the captain was about to signal for an increase to thirty knots when he felt a slight shutter through the control console. He paused, slowly turning toward the First Officer. Just as he was about to speak, a second shutter occurred, followed by a third. The ship was slowing rapidly as if caught in sludge.

The *Norwegian Classic* was Aarzam's 'second cut'.

At the same moment, the ship's intercom began to come alive as crewman down below screamed alerts about the rush of ocean water now surging into the ship as a result of the explosions of the underwater mines.

Of the five mines placed below the keel, only three had detonated. The flood pumps could not keep up with the flow of incoming water, resulting in the ship listing to the left. In addition, most of the damage occurred to the rear half of the ship, causing the stern to begin sinking in the water.

S-O-S messages were sent on all naval frequencies to maximize both ship and shore response. Within five minutes, the order to launch lifeboats was given; however, by the time the crew was properly positioned, ten minutes had passed.

Now, it was a race against time. The rush of water filled the bowels of the ship – the ship was listing to port – the stern lowering in the water – the lifeboats being lowered – people running without direction – people were pushed overboard by the crowd surging toward the nearest lifeboat.

The Captain called the ship's radio office. "Have we had any response to our S-O-S?!" "Two ships acknowledged our requests for help but have not sent their positions or estimated times of arrival" came the reply.

The Navigator approached the captain. "Sir, here are our coordinates" as he handed the paper to the senior officer.

41°45'59.99" N -50°13'60.00" W

The captain, whose white hair underpinned his many years at sea, immediately recognized the coordinates. They were the same as the RMS Titanic on that fateful day in April, 1912 when more than 1,500 people were lost after the ship hit an iceberg.

He returned his gaze to the navigator, who had also recognized the coincidence. "I know" was the quiet response from the junior officer. "This isn't going to happen on my watch" was the captain's firm reply.

Fifteen minutes had now transpired since the first explosion. The first of the lifeboats were just now contacting the water as the ship continued to list to port and slowly sink at the stern.

In an attempt to rally his crew on the bridge, the captain loudly proclaimed "We're going to make it! Tend to your duties and keep this ship afloat! We're not losing anyone on my watch!"

The crew's spirits were bolstered by the captain's words. As they began to quicken their pace, news came from the engine room that the crew was getting the upper hand on the flooding. As they pumped water toward the bow to relieve the sinking of the stern, they were also able to arrest the listing to port.

The ship was stabilized. The captain began to smile. *'We're going to make it'* he thought.

At that moment, the radio operator called up to the bridge. "Tell the captain that the *HMS Queen Elizabeth* has indicated their arrival on station in 24 hours. The ULCC *Kellingsly* is closer and can be here in six hours."

As the good news was relayed to the captain, he gave a shout and a raised fist as a victory gesture. "Help's coming lads! Let's stay focused, protect the passengers, and all go home safely!" he thundered.

*What was it?* the captain thought. *What was it that injured his ship? Had they hit some underwater object? There were no charted sea mounds in this area. There were no reports of submerged icebergs. Any potential clash with a submarine would be infinitesimal given a sub's advanced electronics. What was it? A bomb? But, why would anyone want to bomb a cruise ship?* Nothing made any sense.

As he was deep in thought, the chief engineer emerged from the stairway leading to the engine room. "Sir, can we speak in private?" was his quiet message to the captain.

The captain led the way to his stateroom and closed the door behind them. "What is it, Chief?"

The Chief began his report. "Sir, you may think I'm crazy. But, I had our emergency dive team enter into the bilge area of the damaged sections of the hull in an effort to ascertain the extent of our damage. They have reported that the ruptured portions of the hull were not caused by a tear in the structure, as if we had collided with a submerged object. Rather, they told me that the metal was bent inward as if from an exterior explosion.

Sir, they believe that we are a victim of multiple mine explosions along portions of the hull. And, given the location of the penetrations, they believe there are other mines still out there that haven't detonated yet. Someone wanted to take out the entire bottom of the ship so that we would sink in less than one minute! The divers want permission to make an exterior hull dive to look for more explosives. We may have stabilized a minimal level of buoyancy for now but, if there are more, and they detonate, we'll sink like a rock in less than one minute."

The captain slowly sat in his chair, a perplexed look crossing his face. "Why would someone want to sink our ship in such a catastrophic manner?" he wondered aloud.

He thought for a few more seconds and then responded. "Get the divers in the water quickly. If there are more mines attached to the hull, we have to get them detached as quickly as possible before the ULCC *Kellingsly* gets close to us. If their oil cargo were to detonate, it would destroy everything within 1,000 meters of our location. Did you hear about the ULCC that exploded in Victoria Harbor two days ago?"

"I heard" the chief replied as he turned to leave the stateroom. "I'll have the divers in the water in five minutes."

"Make it three minutes!" the captain called out.

1D.10 Response to Second Cut

\* \* \* \* \* \* \* \* \* \* \* \* \* \* \* \* \* \* \* \* \* \* \* \* \* \* \*

Clancy was still staring at the world map when the nearby elevator doors opened, revealing his intelligence officer exiting the paneled enclosure.

"Clancy, I've got something for you to see" he remarked in his trademark monotone voice. As he handed a summary report to Clancy, he began remarking on its content.

"Sir, we have just intercepted emergency radio traffic from the *Norwegian Classic,* a large passenger luxury liner currently transiting the Atlantic Ocean. They are currently taking on water due to experiencing several explosions."

Clancy looked up from the report. "How did you happen to pick up their emergency signal?"

The intelligence officer moved closer to the map and began pointing with his finger. "We think their position is here" he tapped with his finger "just about the same location as where the Titanic went down in the North Atlantic. They made a broadcast on 406 MHz, which is the internationally recognized distress frequency monitored in the U.S. by National Oceanic and Atmospheric Administration, the Air Force Rescue Coordination Center, and the United States Coast Guard. The signal is sent to a network of American, Russian, Canadian and French weather and global navigation system satellites that are part of the COSPAS-SARSAT international satellite-based search and rescue system."[4]

"How many people are on board?" Clancy inquired.

"The ship is spec'd out at 5,000 passengers" the officer replied.

Clancy followed-up. "Are they asking for our assistance?"

"Not at this time. It appears the ULCC *Kellingsly* has diverted from their intended route to intercept the *Norwegian Classic* and provide assistance. The Royal Navy has also been contacted and indicated they have a naval warship enroute to the scene."

The young communications officer renewed his earlier observation. "Sir, this has got to be *IWO*!

His hand still on his chin, Clancy again returned his gaze to the world map. *The ULCC Lockerman in Victoria Harbor and, now, the Norwegian Classic in the North Atlantic. This is too coincidental.*

Turning to his intelligence officer, Clancy barked "Get the staff into the conference room in thirty minutes. Have them bring all up-to-date information they have on *IWO's* known and rumored operations. Contact our counterintelligence chief and have him participate via conference call. I don't want to get caught flat-footed if *IWO* is making a move!"

1D.11 False Hope

\* \* \* \* \* \* \* \* \* \* \* \* \* \* \* \* \* \* \* \* \* \* \* \* \* \*

The *HMS Queen Elizabeth (QE)* had been in port at Portsmouth, having returned from sea trials conducted to test a new propeller design. Following initial evaluations, they had put to sea again for Phase Two of their trials when the distress call from the *Norwegian Classic* was received.

"All ahead flank!" was the HMS QE's captain. "I want to get to them ahead of schedule!" Within one minute, the large aircraft carrier began surging through the water at their classified speed of thirty knots.

The ULCC *Kellingsly* was closer to the *Norwegian Classic*. Unfortunately, at over 1,500 feet in length and holding more than 3,000,000 barrels of oil from the Middle East, its top speed of sixteen knots was far less than naval vessels. Nonetheless, the *Kellingsly's* captain also ordered top speed for his vessel.

"With any luck, we'll get there in time to save everyone aboard" the captain said as he turned toward his second officer. "It will be fortunate that we will arrive while it is still daylight" came the reply.

Back aboard the *Norwegian Classic*, the captain had given the order to cease all lifeboat activity. Now that the ship had been stabilized and the listing to port was beginning to reduce, he felt it was safer for passengers to remain aboard rather than be bounced around in the ocean waves aboard small lifeboats.

Meanwhile, Aarzam's phone rang. His agent in Iceland, who had sent the radio signal to detonate the mines on the bottom of the *Norwegian Classic,* was on the other end.

"Aarzam, we've been monitoring the naval radio traffic and heard that the *HMS Queen Elizabeth* and the ULCC *Kellingsly* picked up the distress call from the *Norwegian Classic.* They are due to arrive on scene at twenty-four and six hours, respectfully. What would like me to do?"

"Why didn't the cruise ship sink immediately?!" thundered Aarzam.

"The mines sold to us by the Russians were an older variant and, therefore, less reliable. As near as we can tell, at least two or three of the mines detonated."

Aarzam thought for a moment then responded. "Can we order the sequence of the mine detonation?"

"Not really" was the reply. "All of the mines on each ship were set to the same radio signal. When we send the signal, all of them should detonate at the same time."

Although Aarzam's original plan was to destroy the Chinese aircraft carrier *Liaoning* as it was putting to sea from its base at the Yulin Naval Base located on Hainan Island in the South China Sea, he was overjoyed at the prospect of destroying both an ULCC oil tanker and a British aircraft carrier at the same time.

"Okay" was Aarzam's reply. "Wait until both the oil tanker and the English aircraft carrier are on scene at the same time. Monitor the radio traffic and detonate the mines on both of those ships during the height of the rescue. And try to send the signal again to the mines on the cruise ship. I want all three ships on the bottom of the ocean!"

After four more hours, the ULCC *Kellingsly* was now within visual range of the *Norwegian Classic*. Passengers and crew alike on the cruise ship let out shouts of joy at the sight of the mammoth oil tanker emerging from the horizon.

Aboard the *HMS Queen Elizabeth*, the Combat Information Center Watch Officer (CICWO) emerged from the Combat Information Center (CIC) where he had been monitoring the plight of the *Norwegian Classic* and the proximity of the ULCC *Kellingsly*. He made his way up to the bridge to inform the captain of the current situation.

"Sir," he began "the ULCC *Kellingsly* has the cruise ship in sight and is now maneuvering to a position adjacent to the *Norwegian Classic* to lend support. They are attempting to use their array of ballast and oil transfer pumps to relieve water from flooded compartments in order to increase the buoyancy of the cruise ship. The water is calm and they feel the risk is low at this point."

"Very well" replied the captain. "How far are we along?"

The CICWO followed-up. "The navigator is estimating that we should arrive a little more than sixteen hours, which will place us four hours ahead of schedule."

The captain gave a quizzical look to the CICWO since this new estimate reflected a speed faster than the *HMS Queen Elizabeth* could travel.

Noticing the expression on the captain's face, the CICWO responded. "He was apparently extra conservative in his original estimate. I think he padded the numbers to ensure we would arrive on scene ahead of schedule . . . in deference to your stated desire to do so when we were assigned this mission."

The captain smiled and let out a brief chuckle. "Let's launch a reconnaissance aircraft so we can see what we will be dealing with."

"Aye, Aye, sir" was the response as the CICWO wheeled away toward flight operations.

After another hour had passed, the ULCC *Kellingsly* was now one mile away from the *Norwegian Classic*. But, even at that that distance, the enormity of the tanker was mind boggling. Five hundred feet longer than the Eiffel Tower in Paris, the *Kellingsly* seemed to consume the ocean. And, while there were many advantages of an oil tanker being of such a size, there was also the disadvantage of not being agile in its movements. Thus, great care had to be taken to maneuver slowly during the last mile to control the momentum of this leviathan. Positioning itself adjacent to the cruise ship in order to render assistance would be a task that would take several hours.

It was during the middle of this maneuvering operation that the noise of a British AV-8B Harrier jet passing closely overhead caught everyone's attention. As it circled for another pass and wagged its wings, the cruise ship passengers and crew let another round of shouts for joy at the promise that their ordeal would soon be over.

"Elizabeth, this is Badger One" radioed the reconnaissance pilot. "I am on target."

"Give us the rundown" radioed the CICWO.

The pilot continued. "The ocean is calm and the *Norwegian Classic* appears to be stable. It is listing about ten degrees to port and is down in the water. I estimate that its lower deck is about ten feet above the surface. The *Kellingsly* appears to be maneuvering for a position alongside and is roughly one-half mile on the port side of the *Norwegian*. I see two tender boats in the water . . . numerous passengers on deck."

"Roger, Badger One. I'm sure the sight of your aircraft is providing comfort to the crew and passengers. Remain on station. Keep us apprised of your fuel reserves" replied the CICWO.

"Wilco" responded the pilot.

It took the ULCC *Kellingsly* longer than anticipated to maneuver alongside of the *Norwegian Classic*. After six hours, they were finally in position with mooring lines in place to prevent the ships from drifting apart while maneuvering thrusters kept them from colliding.

While this had been occurring, crewmen from the *Kellingsly* had used several tender boats to ferry medical personnel and supplies to the cruise ship for those who had been injured in the bomb blasts. In addition, they would assist in facilitating the use of the *Kellingsly's* ballast and oil transfer pumps to aid in removing sea water from the *Norwegian Classic's* damaged hull.

It took another four hours to connect the pumps and begin pumping water. At the sight of the sea water being pumped overboard, the passengers and crew let out a shout of joy in their apparent salvation. In spite of the harrowing event, they began to relax and take in some welcome rest as the moon rose over the still ocean.

## 1D.12 Abbas' Countermeasures

\* \* \* \* \* \* \* \* \* \* \* \* \* \* \* \* \* \* \* \* \* \* \* \* \* \*

The small white pickup had seen better days, but the miscellaneous dents, scratches, and dirt allowed it to blend in with the other small white pickups travelling the dusty roads.

Abbas was still light-headed from the explosions in Harjiwan. The ringing in his ears continued and his vision remained blurry but was slowly improving. His head hurt, probably the result of a concussion from the blast.

He had to speak with Arthur. His sixth sense was telling him that the conflict between *IWO* and the Western Alliance was either imminent or had already begun. He failed in placing too much faith in Aarzam. Abbas couldn't be sure if the attack at Harjiwan originated from the Western Alliance or from Aarzam's intelligence operatives in *IWO*.

In either case, it was imperative that he attempt to bring the promise of a conflict to a halt. Arthur had been successful in convincing him of the futility of the war they had both strived to prepare for.

He drove a circuitous route toward his personal residence, careful to observe the surroundings, in the event his home was under surveillance. Not seeing anyone, other than local children from the neighborhood, he parked the truck one block away from the rear entrance to his home.

His senses were returning to him as he made his way along the alley behind his house. Stopping by a telephone pole, he reached down and lifted a small, nondescript rock. Underneath was a metal tin from which he removed a pocket-sized 9mm semiautomatic pistol and a key to the back door of his house.

He slowly approached the door, looking for telltale signs of footprints left behind from someone who may have booby-trapped his home. Not seeing anything out of the ordinary, he inserted the key into the lock and slowly opened the door, pistol in hand, looking for any attached wires that might portend the existence of a small explosive device. None could be seen.

He closed the door quietly and began a room-by-room search of his residence. All appeared as it was when he was last here with Rasha.

Returning to the kitchen, he placed the pistol on the table and opened a drawer revealing several spare cell phones. All needed charging so he selected one and connected it to the nearest outlet.

The weariness of the day was catching up with him. Knowing it would be an hour before he would have sufficient charge on the phone to begin the many conversations he needed to have, he made his way to the bathroom and collapsed on the shower floor, grateful to be able to rest in the innocence of the rain-like water cascading down upon him.

Abbas awoke with a start. He found himself on the floor of his shower which was now spewing cold water. Taking a few seconds to orient himself, he leaped to his feet, peered down the hallway toward the kitchen, and slowly made his way through family room toward the pistol on the table.

Picking up the weapon gave him a sense of comfort; now he could defend himself against any of Aarzam's intruders should they show up at his home.

He glanced at the phone and saw that it was nearly 75% charged. But, who to call first?

He was in need of reinforcements – people loyal to him who could provide a current assessment of what had been happening in his absence.

He also needed to speak with Arthur. It was imperative that he kept the peace dialogue open.

Abbas picked up his phone and began to dial.

## 1D.13 The Dig Continues

\* \* \* \* \* \* \* \* \* \* \* \* \* \* \* \* \* \* \* \* \* \* \* \* \* \* \* \*

The loss of Frank's contribution to the Arab-Israeli archaeology dig at Nahsholim was monumental. Nonetheless, the IMA and EMA Directors were concerned that continued existence of the dig effort needed to be secured.

Accordingly, they made the decision to travel to Jerusalem to meet with members of the Knesset. It was imperative they obtain permission to continue the dig under the protection of the Israeli military.

As it turned out, the Knesset was on a break between sessions when the two Directors walked into the Prime Minister's office to appeal for his support.

"Sir" the IMA Director began, in addition to the brave soldiers that were lost in the recent attack at Nahsholim, there were a number of archaeology staff injured. Unfortunately, our lead archaeologist, an American, succumbed to his wounds and died just a short while ago."

The Prime Minister was moved with compassion, not only for the loss of the soldiers, but for the Director's loss as well. He stood up and walked from behind his desk and gave the IMA Director a brotherly hug.

Shaking hands with the EMA Director, he responded

"We have all lost great treasures this day. You, the loss of your archaeology comrade and, me, the future of our country, those who willingly put on a uniform and risk their lives for the rest of us."

"But," he continued "we remain strong as a way of honoring their sacrifice. Earlier today, when the Knesset was informed of the attack, one member rose to his feet and reminded us that we cannot let terrorists dictate how we run our country or efforts aimed at uncovering the history of our country; that, we should double our efforts to re-open the dig site as quickly as possible. It is important for the world to see that we will not be intimidated by criminal acts!

Therefore, as we speak, Colonel Beagan is putting together a new defensive force that will be stationed at Nahsholim tomorrow. His sole objective is to ensure the safety of the site. I encourage you to return to Nahsholim this evening so that preparations can be made to reopen the site as quickly as possible. No one, and I mean no one, will deter us in our quest to uncover the history of our nation!"

The two Directors were dumbfounded, not expecting their archaeological mission to be so warmly embraced, in light of the terrorist attack.

"You are so kind to honor us with your support" responded the EMA Director. "It may seem callous to others that we focus our attention on our work as opposed to mourning over the loss of our colleague. But, I know that Frank wouldn't have it any other way. And, by continuing the dig, we keep his memory alive."

"Excellent!" replied the Prime Minister. "I will let Colonel Beagan know to expect you this evening. With the additional military personnel being assigned to the dig, you should have the resources you need to complete the necessary cleanup in order for your scientific work to continue."

The men walked into the hallway and parted ways; the Prime Minister making his way to the Knesset chambers while the two Directors walked in the opposite direction to a waiting armored personnel carrier that would see them safely to Nahsholim.

While they were excited to return and reopen the dig site, they were also worried about how many of the dig team members would return to their work.

None had signed up for this type of danger.

# T+2 Day

2D.1 Third Cut

\* \* \* \* \* \* \* \* \* \* \* \* \* \* \* \* \* \* \* \* \* \* \* \* \* \* \*

At 7:00am the following morning, the *Norwegian Classic's* lookout quickly communicated over the intercom to the bridge "There she is!  Wow, what a beautiful sight!  British warship off the starboard quarter at 090 degrees!"

The Officer of the Watch quickly walked out the starboard hatchway onto the flying bridge.  Raising his binoculars to look in the direction given, there she was – the *HMS Queen Elizabeth,* Great Britain's newest aircraft carrier.  "Tell the captain that the Royal Navy has arrived" he ordered the yeoman standing nearby.  At once, the young seaman disappeared, hastily making his way to the Captain's cabin.

Three minutes later, the captain was on the bridge admiring the same sight.  Still ten miles away, the carrier still loomed large on the water.  Unable to contain his excitement, he picked up the microphone for the public address (PA) system.

"Ladies and gentlemen of the *Norwegian Classic*, Good Morning!  I know it is early, but it gives me great pleasure to inform you that the Royal Navy has arrived.  When you get up on deck, make your way to the right side of the ship and feast your eyes on one of the most beautiful sights you will ever witness!"

Passengers had been too excited to sleep in, so most were in the ship's dining room eating breakfast when they heard the captain's announcement.  As if responding to a fire drill, they leaped from their seats, chairs falling backward, and made their way toward the windows and doorways on the right side of the ship.

There, steaming toward them was the pride of the British fleet, along with several missile cruisers and destroyers. It seemed as though the entire British navy had come to the rescue. As if on command, everyone began to shout for joy at the prospect of their imminent rescue.

"Ladies and gentlemen, if I could have your attention" came the captain's voice over the PA system once again. To allow for an orderly transfer to the navy ships, I would ask that you return to your cabins and select clothing you will wear for today and one change of clothes. The rest of your luggage will have to remain on board the *Norwegian Classic*. The navy ships will be unable to accommodate your belongings. You will be limited to one suitcase per family, so be judicious in your selection of personal belongings. As we get close to the time of debarkation, the crew will begin to organize passengers on the boat deck for ferrying over to the naval vessels. We have a couple of hours before this occurs, so please us this time wisely."

As passengers moved toward their cabins, the excited conversations revolved around leaving the *Norwegian Classic and getting to sail on a British warship.* They were trading one adventure for another!

Or so they thought . . .

After two hours, passengers had returned to the boat deck where crewmen had organized them into groups of three hundred, the number of people each motorize lifeboat could accommodate.

Navy launch boats were in the water as a safety precaution when the first of the lifeboats began to be lowered into the water. One by one, they entered the water and began making their way toward three Navy destroyers that had moved to within 500 meters of the stricken cruise ship.

Since the *Kellingsly* was positioned on the port side of the *Norwegian Classic,* continuing its pumping operations, the port side lifeboats were unusable. This meant only half the passengers could be offloaded at one time. Once delivered to the naval vessels, the lifeboats would return to gather the remaining passengers.

All was proceeding smoothly. Ten lifeboats were now making their way toward the three Navy destroyers. The *HMS Queen Elizabeth* had weighed anchor while the remaining ships in her armada were now sailing in a wide circular pattern around the *Norwegian Classic* and the *Kellingsly.*

Aboard one of the lifeboats, one small child was wide-eyed at the large naval vessels now looming close. "Oooh!" he exclaimed. He pulled on his mother's arm and pointed. "Look mommy! That one made bubbles in the water like I sometimes do in the bathtub!"

His mother smiled, embarrassed by the public outburst of her young son while she looked in the direction of his pointed finger.

Her smile turned into a look of horror as the terrorist mines attached to the hull of the *HMS Queen Elizabeth* detonated. The bubbles in the water transformed into geysers reaching several hundred meters into the air. In a split second, the sound of the explosions reached the people in the enclosed lifeboat.

They screamed in terror as the large aircraft carrier began to sink in the water. Sailors on deck were seen running in all directions, caught off guard by an emergency for which they had never trained. In two minutes, the ocean washed over her flight deck and, in another two minutes, she vanished from sight, taking most of her 4,000 crewmen below the waves.

In another lifeboat, passengers were watching a similar scene unfold as the mines attached to the *Kellingsly* detonated, causing the same geysers of water. And, as with the ULCC *Lockerman* in Hong Kong's Victoria Harbor a few days prior, the morning sky lit up with detonation of *Kellingsly's* three million barrels of oil. The ship seemed to leap out of the water and, at the same time, disappeared from view as the surrounding sea created a plume of water that totally obscured the tanker.

The force of the explosion created fireball that rose 1,000 feet into the air. Already weakened from her own damage, the *Norwegian Classic* capsized. Five of the lifeboats that were still close to the cruise ship also capsized from the small tidal wave emanating from the blast of the *Kellingsly's* explosion. Even the naval vessels, designed to handle rough seas, bobbed up and down like toy boats being buffeted by waves on a lake.

Aarzam's third cut.

## 2D.2 Response to Third Cut

\* \* \* \* \* \* \* \* \* \* \* \* \* \* \* \* \* \* \* \* \* \* \* \* \* \*

Clancy and his staff were reviewing their plans from the preceding afternoon when the conference room phone rang. The intelligence officer picked up the receiver, listened momentarily, then handed the phone to Clancy. "It's the Admiral Smythe from the Royal Navy."

Clancy looked surprised having not expected the call. With a quizzical look on his face, he took the phone. "Admiral, what can I do for you this morning?"

"Have you been monitoring the events of the last 48 hours!" the admiral shouted.

While Clancy was aware of major developments that had occurred from the attack on Abbas to the sinking of the two ships, he was taken aback by the harsh tone of the admiral and turned on his natural defensive posture. "What do you think you know that I don't!" Clancy shouted back.

The admiral continued his tirade. "I'll tell you what! We just lost *HMS Queen Elizabeth!* From the time we received the distress call, she sank in just four minutes! And, along with her, were the ULCC *Kellingsly* and the passenger liner *Norwegian Classic!* All three ships sunk in less than ten minutes! This has *IWO* written all over it! The Prime Minister and I want to know what you're doing about it!"

Clancy was dumbfounded. *How could IWO have coordinated attacks on three different types of vessels in such a short period of time . . . at the same location . . . at the same time?*

Although it seemed like minutes, only a few seconds passed as he contemplated his next move. "I have been working with my staff on counterstrike plans for the last two days and they are ready. I have also pre-positioned Western Alliance military assets around the globe for a rapid, global response. We're ready and we're attacking, Admiral! Keep me posted on your rescue operations."

Clancy hung up the phone. Everyone in the room was silent as they stared at Clancy for details of the call, having heard the shouting that had occurred on both ends of the phone call.

Clancy looked up at the expectant facial expressions. "*IWO* is on the offensive! They have apparently sunk the *HMS Queen Elizabeth,* the ULCC *Kellingsly,* and the passenger liner *Norwegian Classic!* And, they did it all at the same time when the ships were out in the middle of the ocean! Now, I knew they had a rudimentary yet effective communication capability. What I did not know was that their command-and-control structure was this sophisticated! Let's mobilize the Western Alliance forces for a counterstrike! Get me the operational commanders on a joint conference call so we can launch simultaneous attacks."

Clancy paused; his officers were not rising from the table fast enough. "NOW, people!" he shouted for emphasis. The staff scattered from the conference room to their pre-assigned workstations for conducting wartime operations.

Clancy turned, looked out the window, and smiled. He finally had the war he had so desperately wanted. And the beauty of it was that *IWO* had made the first strike; his hands would be 'clean' from accusations of being a warmonger.

He turned toward the battle maps he had been reviewing when the British admiral had called when his phone rang once again. His intelligence officer picked up the receiver, listened momentarily, then handed the phone to Clancy. "It's the Admiral Yuen from the Chinese Navy."

*What does this guy want?!* thought Clancy.

Clancy took the receiver and greeted the admiral. "Good morning admiral. What can I do for you today?" Not knowing Admiral Yuen, Clancy spoke slowly in the event the admiral's knowledge of English was lacking. However, Admiral Yuen, having been educated in the England, responded in perfect grammar and enunciation.

"General, I would like to know why you attacked and sunk the *Liaoning*, the flagship of our fleet and our prized aircraft carrier!"

Clancy wasn't prepared for this. His first response was to be defensive.

"What are you talking about? We're allies! Why would you think that we would attack one of your ships?!"

"Because" shouted the admiral, "the *Liaoning* had just departed from its home port at the Yulin Naval Base in the South China Sea! Because you have ships in the South China Sea conducting live fire exercises! Because news outlets are reporting that several of your anti-ship missiles went astray and into our aircraft carrier! We lost 3,000 sailors when the ship went down! There were no survivors! Give me a reason why China shouldn't leave the Western Alliance and join with *IWO* against the West!"

Clancy was dumbfounded. First Admiral Smythe calls to confirm the sinking of the ULCC *Kellingsly,* the passenger liner *Norwegian Classic*, and the loss of the *HMS Queen Elizabeth*. Now, Admiral Yuen is talking about the sinking of the *Liaoning*!

"Admiral," Clancy responded "I just received a similar phone call from Admiral Smythe of the Royal Navy. He confirmed the sinking of the ULCC *Kellingsly,* the passenger liner *Norwegian Classic*, and the loss of the *HMS Queen Elizabeth* in the Atlantic. We both agreed that the disparate nature of these attacks is consistent with other assaults being carried out by *IWO*. In the case of other ships, they were sunk with the use of underwater mines placed against the hulls. I would venture to guess that, if you send dive teams to the site of the *Liaoning's* sinking, you will find evidence of underwater detonations, not surface level missile damage."

There was silence on the other end of the phone.

After a few seconds, Admiral Yuen spoke in a quieter but determined voice. "I will follow-up on your recommendation to investigate the hull damage on the *Liaoning*. But know this general – if I don't find evidence of any damage by mines, I will petition my government to withdraw from the Western Alliance and declare war on the West. None of your ships will be safe!"

The phone line went abruptly dead, denying Clancy the opportunity to voice his anger against the admiral's threat. Clancy slammed the phone back onto the receiver and glared at his intelligence officer.

Then, he slowly turned toward the window and smiled. Clancy would use all of *IWO's* terrorist activities to build momentum among the Western Alliance to justify a harsh response.

*Now,* he thought, *he could counterstrike with impunity and send IWO back to the Stone Age!*

## 2D.3 Fourth Cut

\* \* \* \* \* \* \* \* \* \* \* \* \* \* \* \* \* \* \* \* \* \* \* \* \*

Aarzam smiled.

Abbas' original strategic plan of creating mass confusion as to mask *IWO's* movements around the world had been brilliant. While it was exciting to blow up ships, the unexpected detonation of car bombs around the world in a haphazard manner was a terrorist's dream-come-true because it would have the effect of putting all infidels on edge. The impact of the combination of both physical and psychological warfare would sow discord and fear among the countries of the Western Alliance.

Forty-eight hours earlier, he had instructed his young protégé, Achmed, to select 10,000 cars for detonation over the next 72-hour period, from varying regions around the globe, including regions occupied by Muslims.

"Achmed!" Aarzam shouted loud enough to be heard outside of his office. In a few seconds, the young officer entered Aarzam's office. Do you have your automobile targeting list ready to go?

The young man quickly responded "Yes sir!"

"Alright then, make it happen" Aarzam concluded. "Remember to spread out the random detonations over the next 72 hours."

The young officer, still beaming at having been given such a great responsibility, quickly turned and left the room.

* * * * * * * * * * * * * * * * * * * * * * * * * *

The young couple had just parked their car in Wembley's Barham Park, just northwest of London. They beamed as they walked around their new automobile, the result of numerous years of saving all of their spare money. Their friends had met them at the park to help celebrate their new purchase with a day of fun and relaxation.

All were crowded around the shiny specimen of automobile engineering when the explosive, secreted within the rear quarter-panel, detonated. With the nearly simultaneous detonation of the car's fuel tank, the resultant fireball created an image reminiscent of a distant battlefield. Within a fraction of a second, they were all gone, having been consumed by flaming gasoline or disintegrated by shrapnel.

Elsewhere in London and surrounding communities, the repetitive detonation of other vehicle explosives created havoc not seen since the blitz attacks of World War II.

Along the Quai de Grenelle in Paris, numerous new taxis exploded within seconds of one another, erasing nearby tourists from adjacent sidewalks leading to the Eiffel Tower.

* * * * * * * * * * * * * * * * * * * * * * * * * *

Approximately one hour later, Aarzam's intelligence chief came into his office. "Aarzam, you need to come out here and see this!"

Aarzam rose from his chair followed the intelligence officer to a large screen television in the outer office. Images of the aftermath of automobile explosions were occurring in Europe, North America, and the Far East.

The young protégé let out a shout of excitement at the confusion he was witnessing on television. Networks were showing video footage of blackened, smoking automobile frames appearing in municipalities in Europe. Bodies strewn about, destroyed buildings, crumpled bicycles, car pileups on freeways, and burning homes filled the screen as observers attempted to rationalize the scenes of horror unfolding in their communities.

Aarzam's fourth cut.

## 2D.4 Response to Fourth Cut

\* \* \* \* \* \* \* \* \* \* \* \* \* \* \* \* \* \* \* \* \* \* \* \* \* \*

Clancy stared out the window as he waited for the Western Alliance Forces Command conference call to be arranged for coordinating his first strike against *IWO*. He was somewhat jealous that *IWO* had made the first move as he would have preferred to have caught them off-guard with a surprise pre-emptive strike. Nonetheless, *IWO* being the aggressor took the burden off his shoulders with regards to launching a powerful counterstrike. He could now defend nearly anything he did going forward as a defensive response to *IWO's* aggression.

He was lost in thought when his communications officer reentered the conference room. Walking purposefully toward the television, he called out to Clancy "Sir, you've got to see this!"

Clancy turned just as the news channel was rebroadcasting video of the aftermath of numerous car explosions occurring around the world. The announcer could barely contain her emotions.

> *"We have reports that multiple car explosions have just occurred in London. First responders are reporting over 1,000 casualties so far. Our . . . just a moment please . . . okay, my producer is telling me that we have information from our affiliate station in Paris. Go ahead Patrice."*

*"Carol, we are getting reports of multiple car explosions here in Paris and in small towns across the country. Over 2,000 thousand people have been killed just in Paris alone. There doesn't seem to be any rhyme or reason in these attacks. No terrorist groups have claimed responsibility yet, so we don't know where to focus our attention. Wait . . . I am sending you to our New York bureau. Go ahead, Patrick."*

*"Patrice, police in New York, Washington DC, and Atlanta are reporting numerous car explosions all over their cities. While we don't have a full count yet, they are estimating up to five thousand people injured or killed. It would appear that we are experiencing the same catastrophe here that is occurring in Europe. Wait . . . we are just now getting initial reports from St. Louis that the same type of car explosions are occurring in their city. These attacks appear to have begun in Europe and are moving west across the globe."*

Clancy's mind began to churn, drowning out the news reporters. *How could IWO have pulled off simultaneous car explosions on a global basis?! The logistics that would have been required would have taken months, if not years to pull this off!*

*But, he killed Abbas in the drone strike. So, this must be part of a battle plan Abbas developed some time ago and is now being carried out by his staff.*

Clancy paused in thought.

*Aarzam!*

*Of course. This had to be the work of Aarzam. Intelligence had always maintained that he was the loose cannon in Abbas' staff. Fathi was too unrefined and Sayyid was too much of a traditional soldier to fight in this manner.*

*First the ULCC tanker, then the cruise ship, then a naval vessel, and now random automobile explosions around the world.*

*Aarzam was tipping his hand at the strategy developed by Abbas. It contained unconventional attacks, using unconventional weapons, on unconventional targets, on a global basis. The purpose would be to sow confusion and tie up Western Alliance resources in a perpetual emergency response mode, thus delaying any offensive action.*

As much as Clancy disliked *IWO*, he had to admire the innovativeness of Abbas' strategic plan. It was brilliant.

## 2D.5 Fifth Cut

\* \* \* \* \* \* \* \* \* \* \* \* \* \* \* \* \* \* \* \* \* \* \* \* \* \* \*

Aarzam walked over to Achmed and placed his hand on his shoulder. "Achmed, you have done very well! Look at the devastation you have created! It's now time for the second set of detonations to occur. Let's see what confusion you can cause with the explosive devices that were contained within electronic products."

Achmed went to his desk and picked up the phone. Calling his network of insurgents, he gave the command to detonate the small bombs contained within 5,000 electronic devices. He coordinated with each agent to ensure that the detonations would be spread over the next 72 hours.

After another hour had passed, news reports began to appear about unexplained explosions occurring in homes and electronics stores.

As with the automobile explosions, each community treated the incidents as a local issue, unaware of the global nature of similar explosions. It was only those with access to global intelligence services that first began to understand the sinister nature of the seemingly unassociated chaotic events.

Aarzam's fifth cut.

## 2D.6 Response to Fifth Cut

\* \* \* \* \* \* \* \* \* \* \* \* \* \* \* \* \* \* \* \* \* \* \* \* \* \* \* \*

Clancy was about to enter the Command Center's war room to launch his coordinated counterstrike against *IWO* when the next news broadcast came on the television screen.

*"This is Steve reporting from Los Angeles. Not only have massive car explosions been center-stage on the news, we are now receiving reports of numerous building explosions occurring in retail centers. Reports coming in from local police indicate that the preponderance of these explosions have involved stores selling electronic equipment such as television and audio equipment. Patrick, what are you hearing there in New York?"*

*Steve, it's chaos here" replied Patrick. "Authorities are reporting numerous explosions in the retail sectors of the city. Fire departments are responding to multiple calls of house fires caused by unknown explosions. People are afraid to go into buildings or be seen on the sidewalks. Pedestrians are being killed by the hundreds from shrapnel coming from exploding automobiles. Let's pass it over to Patrice in Paris."*

*"Patrick, police are reporting numerous explosions in audio equipment retail stores found in Paris' 10th and 15th Arrondissements (city districts). We are also experiencing a high volume of fire*

*department response to residential locations due to unexplained home explosions, just as you are in America."*

Clancy was transfixed by the television news coverage. In some ways, it was better than his own intelligence network due to the distributed nature of the news media and their instantaneous access to the air waves.

For the first time, Clancy felt as though he was being caught off-guard. *So many successful, disparate attacks in such a short period of time! Aarzam was ratcheting up his operational tempo with yet another offensive! Where was he going to strike next?!*

Clancy continued his mental gymnastics, trying to predict *IWO's* battle plan. He was a traditional soldier who thought in a traditional manner when it came to combat strategy. This overly unconventional approach being adopted by *IWO* was too far removed from his 'look-them-in-the-eyes' style of fighting. He found himself at a total loss attempting to prophesy what *IWO* would do next.

He was so lost in thought that Clancy did not hear the repeated calls for him in the war room. Finally, his intelligence officer exited the room tugged at his arm.

"Sir, we have the operational commanders on the conference line. They've been waiting for several minutes."

Clancy snapped out of his trance and walked briskly into the war-room, his jaw set firmly toward the task of revenge!

Speaking firmly on the video-conference camera, Clancy began a series of command directives.

"Gentlemen, you are aware of the nature of the Alpha Target Package.   It's was designed to accomplish three fast-action objectives.

1) Prioritizing the elimination of *IWO's* command and control structure, both personnel and equipment.
2) The destruction of their major offensive and defensive weapons.
3) The elimination of known large troop concentrations and training camps.

Admiral Smythe, release the B-2 stealth bombers we pre-positioned to begin their bombing runs on IWO's command and control structure. Admiral Torrey – launch your naval aircraft against their offensive and defensive weapons, troop concentrations, and targets of opportunity. General Baxter – reconfigure the orbital paths of your satellites so we can watch the strikes on all Alpha package targets.

IWO has been striking us relentlessly for the past 24 hours.  It's now time we showed them the might of the Western Alliance!  I want all aircraft launched within thirty minutes!"

Admiral Smythe took the opportunity to interject some wisdom into Clancy's battle order.  "Clancy, it's daylight for approximately sixty percent of our Alpha package targets, making them ripe for both visual and radar-guided antiaircraft weapons. Maybe others want to launch in the daylight, but I'm not going to send any Air Force aircraft into a combat situation unless it's by cover of darkness in the wee hours of the morning!"

Clancy fumed. "You'll launch as you were ordered! Don't you grasp the magnitude of the injury IWO has inflicted upon us in the last twenty-four hours!? I want them hit and I want them hit NOW!"

Smythe remained calm. "No, we'll launch against our assigned targets when the probability of high success and minimal allied losses are optimized. For us, that means we'll launch in approximately eight hours. The B-2's are subsonic aircraft and can be easily shot down if we're not careful. We need all of these aircraft to remain flying in order to carry out all of the strikes in the several target packages we have. That means we need them to return home in good working order so we can use them again!"

Admiral Torrey spoke up. "I'm with Smythe. We have the capability to fly at night or in poor weather and reliably hit our targets. For my target packages that are currently in nighttime conditions, I'll launch now. But for those that are in daylight conditions, I'll be delaying those sorties for six to eight hours. I want all my boys to come home so we can maintain a sustainable and repeatable threat to the enemy."

Was this mutiny or common sense? Clancy had difficulty seeing beyond his anger and his overwhelming desire to take the fight to the enemy. Although he hated to admit it, Smythe and Torrey had posited good arguments for delaying their air strikes until the Western Alliance forces had maximum tactical advantage.

"Alright" Clancy retorted. "Launch against all nighttime targets immediately and all other targets as soon as is tactically optimal. Tell your pilots that I want all bombing run video forwarded through their respective CIC's (Combat Information Centers) to Western Alliance headquarters in real-time. I want to be able to monitor our progress. Let's get moving!"

Clancy walked out of the war room and back to his office. While feeling some angst at the thought of *IWO* having claimed the initial momentum in the 'offensive attack' realm, he took solace in having begun the implementation of Arthur's strategic plan for countering *IWO*. The attack order had been given and the first bombs would be dropped in a matter of hours.

Clancy's revenge would soon begin.

But, unbeknownst to Clancy, Smythe and Torrey had pre-arranged their arguments for delaying the West's retaliatory air strikes.

They were working with Arthur.

## 2D.7 Arthur's Countermeasures

\* \* \* \* \* \* \* \* \* \* \* \* \* \* \* \* \* \* \* \* \* \* \* \* \* \*

It was the second day that Arthur and the rest of the Challenger crew had been hiding out at the airstrip near the coastal town of Bahia de los Angeles. In the intervening twenty-four hours, he had been able to make contact with both Admiral Smythe and Admiral Torrey and had been debriefed on the conflict emerging between the Western Alliance and *IWO*. He was dismayed to learn that the shooting war had begun.

He had been studying his original briefing maps and reviewing Internet stories about the unfolding explosions and tragedies occurring around the world when his cell phone rang. "Torrey and Smythe here" was the response as he placed the phone next to his ear.

Torrey began. "Arthur, the situation is escalating fairly rapidly now. We have been able to confirm what you have been reading on the Internet and it appears to be as bad as they are reporting. Lots of civilian deaths and , , , " Smythe broke in " . . . and the loss of the *HMS Queen Elizabeth* and her 4,000 sailors!" Lowering his voice, Smythe continued "My son was on the ship, Arthur." His voice began to crack.

Smythe was stereotypically British. Not one for exaggeration or outward displays of emotion, he was all business when it came to his military career. His effectiveness as a leader on behalf of Great Britain was well known. Arthur knew that this loss was more than professional . . . it was deeply personal.

Arthur responded quietly. "I didn't know that, Smythe. I'm sorry to hear the news. Have you heard from your son? I understand that some crew members were picked up by nearby ships and lifeboats from the *Norwegian Classic.*"

"No, there's been no word. He's not aboard any of the escort destroyers and the *Norwegian Classic* lifeboats have already been collected. They're still searching the area for survivors."

Arthur, urgent to move the dialogue forward in light of the current hostilities, had to rein himself in favor of not appearing insensitive to Smythe's loss. "Let's remain hopeful" was all he could respond with.

Sensing Arthur's pent-up anxiety regarding *IWO*'s initiatives and Clancy's response, Torrey threw Arthur a conversation lifeline. "Gentlemen, I think we need to turn our attention to the matters at hand."

"Quite right you are" responded Smythe. "The longer we postpone, the more time *IWO* has to create more carnage."

Had they been in the same room, Arthur would have given Torrey a wink of thanks. Arthur began. "Has anyone heard from Abbas? Do we have any intelligence to know if he pulled the trigger or was it Aarzam?"

"We've not seen any information, but I should think Butterman would have that information if anyone" Smythe interjected.

"I've been having problems reaching him" responded Arthur. "He went underground a week ago due to a potential threat from Clancy."

Arthur continued. "What about Kruglov or Pao – anyone heard from them?"

"Pao is at his base in Hotan, but I have not heard from him recently" responded Torrey. "But, we do have some bad news regarding Kruglov. He had relocated to his remote base just southeast of the Tbilisi International Airport in Georgia a few days ago. Then, yesterday, the base was hit by Iranian aircraft, essentially flattening the headquarters building and adjacent hangar. They have rescue crews on scene, but no word yet of Kruglov having been found."

"How would the Iranians have found out about his headquarters' location, let alone the fact that he was on the premises?!" Arthur asked incredulously.

Smythe spoke up. "Arthur, my boy, I believe it is high time we realize that Clancy and his lackeys pose as great a risk as does *IWO*. It's time to act."

Torrey chimed in. "Arthur, I know that Clancy has a reputation of being a great field commander. But, I never thought he was content with being an underling. He has been after your job for some period of time and the fact that he tried to have you shot down should be proof enough."

Arthur sighed. "I know what you two are saying. I was on my way back to headquarters to relive him of his duties had we not had the situation of the potential shoot-down of my aircraft. He has control of Western Alliance's formal communication channels, so it makes our job of getting rid of him a little tougher, not to mention the loyalists he has on his side."

"Well, we have a number of loyalists as well" responded Smythe. "In fact, I would surmise that we have a significantly greater number than Clancy spread across multiple countries and branches of service. Because of the network we established, I believe it would be easier to rally them to action easier than you think."

"I agree" inserted Torrey. "I am fully confident that all of my naval commanders are just waiting for you to give the order to act on Clancy's treason and to execute retaliatory strikes against *IWO* for their recent terrorist actions. We have to shock them into ceasing further attacks."

Their positive responses buoyed Arthur's outlook. "Thanks for the input gentlemen. As you were speaking, a plan I have been working on came into sharp focus. Let's see if we can execute it in a timely manner.

Here's what I have in mind."

## 2D.8 Preparing for the Sixth Cut

* * * * * * * * * * * * * * * * * * * * * * * * * *

Aarzam smiled at the bedlam he was witnessing on television among the countries of the world. At this point, he was glad the devastation was involving both infidel and Muslim countries and communities because it served to disguise *IWO* as the instigator of the devastation.

The last group of offensive weapons was comprised of the Russian Vacuum Bombs (RVB's) – a city-block destroyer with a 1,000-foot radius kill zone. He had previously selected an initial group of nine targets: London, Rome, Singapore, Beijing, Saint Petersburg, Atlanta, Brasilia, Tel Aviv, and Riyadh. To ensure that the detonations in this group had a dramatic effect and create the greatest number of casualties, he made the decision to have the first of the nine RVB's detonated at 9:00am local time.

Turning to General Tanzi, Aarzam began "Tanzi, let's begin the detonation of the RVB's tomorrow, keep them two hours apart, and arrange them to occur between the hours of 9:00am and 4:00pm local time. Start with London and work your way westward so that panic will rise as the day progresses."

Tanzi returned to his office and picked up his phone. While he stood viewing a world map marked with small flag pins highlighting the RVB target cities, he began issuing instructions to his team of agents.

A few minutes later, he returned to the large room where *IWO* members were continuing to watch television of the mayhem occurring around the world.

By now, it was late in the afternoon. In London, the first RVB target, it was early evening of the day prior to detonation. Walking up to Aarzam, Tanzi began "I have arranged for the London RVB to detonate first at 9:00a tomorrow. After that, we'll proceed westward and detonate during the target time for each city until the first group is complete."

"Very good!" Aarzam responded. "It's been a great first day for *IWO*! We've put the Western Alliance on their heels and they don't even know it!"

The sixth cut was about to be completed.

2D.9 Target: Pao #2

\* \* \* \* \* \* \* \* \* \* \* \* \* \* \* \* \* \* \* \* \* \* \* \* \* \*

Following the radio conference with Sayyid, the staff at the SSG/IRGC consolidated forces facility in Islamabad worked late into the evening to craft a battle plan for striking Pao at his field headquarters in Hotan, China. Pouring over the satellite images supplied by the double agent, they mapped a route their aircraft could fly to take advantage of the many mountain valleys that would obscure their radar signature.

The final 100 miles would be the most critical. Hotan rested on the northwest edge of the Taklimakan Desert, a vast arid expanse 650 miles long, 275 miles wide, and over 4,200 feet in elevation. The route would take the aircraft over the Karakoram Mountain Range before entering a valley that would lead them to a position southwest of Hotan. They would then enter Chinese airspace over the Taklimakan Desert.

It would be this last 100 miles that would the most dangerous. Even if they could avoid radar, the flatness of the desert would make them visible from a great distance. The only option would be a night attack, using the summer heat rising from the desert floor to aid in masking their engine heat signature.

Their greatest threat would be the surface-to-air missile batteries located at the Hotan base. As the pilots studied the satellite images, they began to realize that they may be flying a one-way mission.

"For *IWO* and Allah!" shouted the young IRGC officer. "For *IWO* and Allah" the pilots and ground crew responded as they turned and jogged out to their aircraft.

It would take the pilots approximately ninety minutes, flying their specified route, to cover the 430 miles to their target. As they lined up on the runway for departure, they were both excited and anxious at what lay ahead. Thoughts of glory were clouded with fear of the unknown.

* * * * * * * * * * * * * * * * * * * * * * * * * *

While the early morning hour should have found him fast asleep, Pao was restless. Although tired from the activity associated with bringing the Hotan base up to combat status, he was finding it difficult to sleep. Arthur's near-death escape from his own forces worried him that the fragile coalition of former rivals, comprising the Western Alliance, may have been overly ambitious.

*Would someone in my command come after me?* he thought. While the recent purge among his military for the missing weapons caches should have both negatively incentivized his people's loyalty and cleaned out any potential opposition, there was always a risk.

The headquarters was quiet as he shuffled softly in his slippers toward the cafeteria for some tea. Guards at their posts in the hallway were shocked to see their supreme military leader walking in his robe in the middle of the night. They hastily snapped to attention as he approached, their memories filled with what happened to their comrades in the recent purge.

Pao found a soft couch and stretched out. From his pocket, he pulled out a copy of one of his favorite book - *The Art of War by Sun Tzu.* Although he had previously read it many times, giving him the ability to quote nearly any passage, he felt that each reading revealed some new nugget of information previously missed.

It was nearly 2:30am when he finally dozed off, having finally reached the point of exhaustion where sleep came in spite of himself.

But the respite was brief.

At 2:50am, the quiet suddenly erupted with the high pitch whine of the air raid sirens. Jolted awake, Pao quickly stood as the headquarters guards rushed into the cafeteria to usher him to the air raid shelter nearby.

The Iranian pilots thought that slowing their airspeed to 300 knots would help to minimize their noise signature from listening posts and flying close to the ground would mask them from enemy radar. But, the night was clear and the desert was flat, two elements that worked against them.

A sentry post, located in the nearby mountain range to the southwest, first caught sight of the Iranian jets as they turned northward from their last canyon. As they called in the first sighting, a second outpost eighty miles south of Hotan confirmed the sighting as the Sukhoi Su-24 jets nearly flew directly overhead. The Iranian pilots were just sixteen minutes from their target.

Unaware they had been spotted, the pilots continued flying straight toward the Chinese base. By now, the missile battery at the Hotan command center had been alerted and the air raid sirens were blaring.

Pao and his escort of guards had reached the air raid shelter with twelve minutes to spare. Having been told the aircraft were approaching at low altitude, Pao ordered the anti-aircraft missile batteries to hold the firing of their missiles until the aircraft were ten miles away. He reasoned that the aircraft were coming in for a low-level bombing run since their minimal altitude was tactically too low for a radar guided missile attack. By delaying the launch of his defensive missiles, he would have a higher probability of luring the pilots into a trap from which they could not escape.

The two Iranian aircraft were only two minutes from their target when the Chinese missile battery commander gave the order to fire. Two missiles from each of three HQ-64[5] launchers were sequentially launched three seconds apart, streaking low above the desert floor in search of their prey. At a top speed of Mach 3, the first missile would reach the two MIG 27's in just 20 seconds.

Although the Iranian pilots immediately detected the missiles being launched through their electronic instruments, there was little they could do. Aggressive flying to avoid the missiles would take them off their flight path and give the Chinese additional opportunities to shoot them down. Staying on course would mean flying into a myriad of missiles and antiaircraft guns.

The lead pilot quickly radioed his wingman "We're less than two minutes out! Dispense flares and chaff, and limit your defensive flying to no more than a ten degree variation from your present course! At the last minute, execute a steep climb while releasing your ordnance! Good luck!"

Both aircraft began aggressive flight maneuvers while dispensing flares and chaff. They felt a sense of welcome victory at being able to avoid the first three missiles. But the last three would not be deterred from their assigned mission.

Reconciling that he would be shot down, the lead pilot yelled through his microphone "Climb fast and release!" Both MIG's rose steeply upward as the fourth missile found the wingman's aircraft. There was just enough time for the lead pilot to see the flash of light before he too was struck by the fifth.

The Iranian pilots had made it to within two miles of the Hotan base.

A great cheer arose from the soldiers on the base who viewed the nighttime light show as if it were a celebration of the Chinese New Year. Rifles were fired into the air as the destroyed jets came crashing to the ground in thunderous explosions.

But the pilots' last maneuver of steeply climbing and simultaneously releasing their ordnance was a method of bombing dating back to World War II. Lobbing a bomb in such a maneuver was a method of bombing a target from a distance that would increase the chances of the attacking aircraft to escape. The bomb would follow a parabolic arc away from the aircraft and toward the target. While an imprecise way of delivering ordnance, it could be effective. Unfortunately, the Iranian jets were too far away and too low for the maneuver to be effective.

As the initial cheers from the soldiers began to fade, there were four large explosions in close succession, noticeably closer than the downed aircraft. The flashes of light immediately halted the cheering. When the sound of the thunder-like explosions reached them seven seconds later, they instinctively jumped back, wondering if other bombs would strike closer.

Military police vehicles sped out of the base toward the downed aircraft in search of the pilots. Chinese intelligence would want to "talk" with them.

After several minutes, the claxon sounded the "All Clear" signal. In fifteen minutes, Pao was informed that the aircraft were Russian MIG 27's with Iranian markings. The pilots were found but not intact.

*The Iranians*? Pao thought. *How would they have known he was at Hotan? Did he have another traitor in his midst or had IWO penetrated his military network?*

He did not stop to consider that his "enemy" might have been an ally in the Western Alliance.

As Pao was crossing the parade grounds towards his quarters, he noticed his military aide running toward him. Chin quickly stopped and saluted, trying hard not to smile at seeing Pao in his bathrobe and slippers.

"Sir," she began "this intercept was just received from Menhinsky, head of Russia's SVR. Kruglov's base in Tbilisi, Georgia was attacked four hours ago by multiple aircraft approaching from the south. The headquarters and hangar facilities were destroyed. Kruglov was on location and his status is unknown at this time. There is a Cold War bunker complex under the headquarters building, but Menhinsky didn't know if Kruglov was able to make it there for safety. They have troops on the ground looking for Kruglov and any survivors."

Pao stared at the piece of paper. *South of Tbilisi was Iran. "Two air attacks emanating from Iran in close succession. Either IWO's intelligence network had penetrated both the Russian and Chinese militaries, or . . . .*

His mind wandered, attempting to consider all possibilities. It was only then that his philosophy came into focus - *Occam's Razor – 'the simplest solution is often the right one'. Could the leak of his and Kruglov's field locations have been the result of traitorous actions on the part of someone within the Western Alliance? But, wait a minute. Wasn't Arthur almost shot down by Clancy? What is the connection between Clancy and IWO?*

Pao turned his stare toward Chin. "I need to speak with Arthur. Set up the call in fifteen minutes."

Pao turned toward his quarters. It was time for the Western Alliance leadership to regain control of the situation.

## 2D.10 Response to Kruglov & Pao Attacks

\* \* \* \* \* \* \* \* \* \* \* \* \* \* \* \* \* \* \* \* \* \* \* \* \* \* \* \*

While Clancy was annoyed with the reservations expressed by Torrey and Smythe, he had to agree with their logic. An excessive loss of offensive air power early in the conflict would be disadvantageous for further strikes.

As he studied the maps on the conference room table, Brannon walked into the room with a paper in his hand. "You've got to see this intelligence report" he stated in a serious tone.

Clancy took the report and began reading. As his eyes scanned down the page, a smile began to cross his face. As he was reading, Brannon came along side and said softly "It looks like your plan worked."

Clancy looked up with the smile that had turned into a grin of accomplishment. "So, Kruglov is now in the great 'Kremlin in the sky'" he waxed poetically. "Any news about Pao?"

Brannon responded in an assured manner. "We have had no reports from Hotan. I would have thought the attacks on both facilities would have been scheduled to occur within proximity of one another, but maybe the China mission was more difficult and is just a little behind. I'll try to find out what's going on over there."

With that, Brannon exited the conference room as Clancy slowly turned to look out the window, slowly rubbing his chin with his hand.

Arthur was still a problem, having escaped the fighter attack a couple of days ago. But, Kruglov was now gone and Pao may shortly follow. That would be two down and one to go. Had it not been for those incompetent fighter pilots, Arthur's plane *would have* been shot down, eliminating the threat against Clancy's ascension to control of the Western Alliance military forces. Then, with Kruglov and Pao dispatched, he would have assumed command of the Western Alliance tomorrow.

*So close, yet so far* he thought.

He stood there for a moment then, looking at his watch, wheeled around and left the conference room.

It was time to check in with Torrey and Smythe.

## 2D.11 Pao & Arthur

\* \* \* \* \* \* \* \* \* \* \* \* \* \* \* \* \* \* \* \* \* \* \* \* \* \* \*

Arthur had just finished his conference call with Torrey and Smythe when his phone rang. The caller ID revealed it was Pao.

His spirits lifted by his prior conversation, Arthur was almost jovial when he answered the call. "Pao, my good friend, I was just planning on calling you. How are things in Hotan?"

Pao, however, was more stoic. "Arthur, I am glad to hear your voice. The last intelligence I received was that Clancy had shot down your aircraft."

"He tried, but I was lucky to have friends in the right places."

Pao continued. "We have several problems. Have you heard about Kruglov?"

"Yes, I was just briefed by Torrey and Smythe. However, I have not received any word of Kruglov's status."

"Neither have I" responded Pao. "I was too busy dodging the enemy aircraft that just attacked my base!"

"Are you okay?! Was anyone injured?!" exclaimed Arthur.

"We shot them down before they could get within striking distance, but they got close . . . about two miles from where I was standing."

"I'm glad you're okay, Pao. Do we know who the attackers were?"

"Iranian, two Sukhoi Su-24 jets. But, I called you about other matters as well. I believe Clancy is somehow in league with *IWO*. It's the only way they could have found out about Kruglov's forward operating base and mine, where we would be, and which buildings to attack. These attack plans were well thought out. In Kruglov's case, there were two flights of two Iranian Sukhoi Su-24 aircraft . . . the very same aircraft that attacked my base."

Arthur thought for a moment. "Sayyid controls the military in Iran. Yet, it's hard to believe he would be so bold and blatantly obvious to conduct such airstrikes on you and Kruglov. I see Aarzam's hand in this somehow."

"That may be," Pao retorted "but the coincidence is too hard to ignore. I have been thinking that *IWO* and our collective use of the same double agents may have been the catalyst from which these attacks sprang. If so, then there is no telling how much other information has been exchanged to our detriment."

"What is your recommendation?" Arthur replied.

"I have a way of dealing with such people in an expeditious manner. I will take care of all of them."

In spite of his desire to tone down the pace at which the conflict had emerged, Arthur knew Pao was taking the Hotan attack personally and yielded to his proclamation.

"Do what you have to do, Pao. I am leaving this in your hands."

The instantaneous click of a phone being hung up was palpable.

# T+3 Day

## 3D.1 Executing the Sixth Cut

\* \* \* \* \* \* \* \* \* \* \* \* \* \* \* \* \* \* \* \* \* \* \* \* \* \*

The sun rose slowly above the eastern horizon, aglow with an orange brilliance. On the western horizon, a waxing crescent moon appeared to glow red as the sun's rays refracted through the Earth's atmosphere. The visual proximity of the planet Mars along the concave portion of the moon resulted in an astronomical representation approximating the crescent and star image found on Islamic flags.

Standing on the balcony of his office, Aarzam stared at the celestial Islamic symbol, convinced that it was a sign from Allah attesting to the success of his military campaign against the Western Alliance.

He was still enthralled with the sight when General Tanzi walked into his Aarzam's office. Turning to see his entry, Aarzam motioned for Tanzi to join him on the balcony. Waving with his arm, Aarzam exclaimed "Tanzi, have you ever seen such a beautiful sight?! It must be a sign from Allah! Our RVB strikes today have been blessed!"

Tanzi was just about to respond when a commotion erupted in the outer office. Turning to view the disturbance, they were greeted by Achmed as he burst through the door.

"Aarzam, you have to come see this!" Achmed shouted as he pointed back over his shoulder toward the large room that served as *IWO*'s central operations center.

Aarzam and Tanzi hurried into the outer office to view the wall monitor Achmed was pointing at. An air assault was being streamed by an *IWO* operative at one of their training and logistics centers housing ordnance and ammunition yet to be distributed to *IWO* forces.

One after another, land-based F-117 Nighthawk stealth aircraft and carrier-based F/A-18 Hornet fighter-bombers were making coordinated, low-level passes in front of the cameraman. The first wave of F-117 aircraft fired air-to-ground missiles designed to destroy radar sites controlling ground-to-air missiles and radar-guided anti-aircraft batteries. The next wave of F/A-18 aircraft released 500-pound bombs on munitions bunkers, creating a cascading series of deafening explosions as each bunker's ordnance detonated.

The third pass was mesmerizing as the cameraman focused on one aircraft approaching from the distance. It was low to the ground, perhaps one hundred feet above the terrain, as it came directly toward the camera. It grew larger in the picture frame as the round silhouette of the fuselage with its wings extended came closer. Then, at the last minute, it swooped upward in a steep arch, revealing its underside and one last bomb being released.

Unfortunately, the cameraman had taken refuge near a wall protecting an ammunition bunker which now had become the prime target for the end of this last aerial attack. The bomb being lobbed toward the cameraman's position seemed to fall in slow motion, transfixing all who were watching the monitor.

Then, the screen went black – the bomb had found its target.

Achmed turned toward Aarzam. "We are getting many reports from our forces that the Western Alliance is counter-attacking on a global basis! We have taken serious losses this morning and they are continuing! It's just one wave after another! Our coastal bases are being attacked by Western Alliance naval ships while land-based installations are being hit with air forces. What are we going to do?!"

Aarzam hesitated. While he always knew that it was just a matter of time before the Western Alliance would counter-attack, the reality of engaging in an actual global conflict was a new experience for him. In the past, his battles had always been local or regional, where the size of the battlefield could be measured in tens of miles and, in most instances, enemy positions were within range of his conventional weapons.

But, to strike at target that was beyond the horizon, and to be struck by an enemy from the same, made the entire experience seem more like a video game being played out on computer monitors.

Snapping back to reality, Aarzam turned toward Tanzi. "Make sure those RVB's detonate on schedule today! That should occupy a substantive number of Western Alliance forces in the resulting disaster relief efforts and dilute their offensive capability."

"I'm on it! London will feel our wrath in about two hours!" was Tanzi's replied as he wheeled about and headed off to his office.

Aarzam returned to his office balcony to see the last of the crescent moon fade away in the brilliant morning sunlight, confident that his impending series of RVB attacks would cripple the West.

Both sides were now shooting . . . the war had begun.

## 3D.2 Response to Sixth Cut

\* \* \* \* \* \* \* \* \* \* \* \* \* \* \* \* \* \* \* \* \* \* \* \* \* \* \*

The schedule for detonating the RVB's had been fixed – each would detonate at 9:00am local time.

> London – GMT (9:00am local time)
> Brasilia - GMT + 3 hours
> Atlanta = GMT + 5 hours
> Beijing – GMT + 16 hours
> Singapore – GMT + 17 hours
> Riyadh – GMT + 20 hours
> Saint Petersburg – GMT + 21 hours
> Tel Aviv – GMT + 22 hours
> Rome – GMT + 23 hours

It was a little after 4:00am when Clancy's phone rang. Having gotten to bed late the night before, he was groggier than usual.

"Hello?" he asked while rubbing the sleep from his eyes.

On the other end was Major Brannon, his intelligence staff officer. "Sir, it's Brannon. They hit London!"

Still rubbing his eyes, Clancy instinctually asked "Who hit London?"

"*IWO!*" Brannon shouted into the phone.

Now, more awake, Clancy wanted details. "Tell me what happened."

Brannon continued.

"Well, given news reports on TV and the corroboration we're receiving from our counterparts in British intelligence, they must have detonated something like a Vacuum Bomb. The surveillance cameras in the area, at what must have been ground zero, were located at the Bank Station, which is near the heart of the financial district. The district cameras went dark at 9:00am local time, which must have been the time of detonation. 9:00am is when most people arrive at work and the streets were crowded with commuter traffic.

Preliminary video is coming in now. It looks like the force of the bomb destroyed everything within a 1,000-foot radius of the blast. They're having great difficulty dealing with the resulting fires due to the amount of debris in the streets along with the casualties.

How would you like to respond?"

Now fully awake, Clancy's first thought was to counter strike with nuclear weapons. "Tell Admiral Smythe I'll be calling him in one hour. And tell him to be ready to outline his nuclear strike plan for execution within three hours! I'll show *IWO* what real destruction is like!" Clancy shouted.

Brannon seemed perplexed that Clancy was not going to the aid of his British allies. "But sir, what about the Brits? Aren't we going to do something to help them in London?"

"Hell no!" Clancy barked. "I've got a nuclear strike to plan and execute. They can take care of themselves!" At that, he slammed the phone down on the receiver and made his way to the shower.

On the other end, Brannon began to worry about what he was going to say to his British colleagues who had just called to follow-up on an earlier request for assistance. Something didn't seem right about Clancy's response. He wondered if the warning about Clancy given to him by Colonel Butterman before he disappeared a week ago was beginning to come to fruition.

Brannon spun on his heels and returned to his office, uncertain what he would tell the British.

## 3D.3 Dig Continues

\* \* \* \* \* \* \* \* \* \* \* \* \* \* \* \* \* \* \* \* \* \* \* \* \* \* \* \*

With support from the Knesset two days ago, workers had already begun repairing the damage from the terrorist attack at the archaeology dig site near Nahsholim.

With Frank dead and Sophie preoccupied with returning his remains to the United States, a leadership vacuum pervaded the team. To fill the void, the IMA Director pleaded with Aaqil and Talibah to assume the role.

"I have shared with you what the Knesset declared just two days ago" stated the IMA Director. "They are insistent that this dig activity continue as a demonstration of Israel's determination not to be intimidated by terrorists. It is vitally important to both us and our Arab friends to continue the work for which so many have given their lives."

Aaqil and Talibah looked at one another, torn between the emotion surrounding the loss of Frank and Sophie and their continuing excitement on what the dig would reveal to the world.

Shuffling his weight from left to right, Aaqil finally broke the silence with a sigh. "Alright, we'll do it." The EMA and IMA Directors smiled and shook hands, relieved the dig would continue under experienced leadership.

Aaqil continued. "But, I want to talk with Colonel Beagan about security so that our continued presence here will not put more lives at risk. We've lost way too many people over the last few days, and I don't want to lose any more."

Talibah turned and began walking toward the tent that had been occupied by Moriah and her students. They had returned to the site to gather their belongings in preparation for their return to the University of Jordan. The young women were packing in silence, each trying to mentally process the events from the last several days.

Moriah felt the need to break the silence. "University is designed to prepare us for life, to expose us to the new and different ideas we will encounter as we begin our adventure as adults. I am sorry this trip has shown you the worst of society."

The women stopped and looked at Moriah. As they stood there, the emotion of the attack, buried during the hyper-activity surrounding the assault and the subsequent events at the hospital, flooded to the surface. Each became teary-eyed as the enormity of their experience suddenly became real: the terrorist attack; the explosions; Moriah still bearing the abrasions from her injuries; Frank's death; Jason's gunshot wound; the death of the Israeli soldiers.

One by one, they crossed the room and hugged Moriah, seeking solace in the arms of an adult who understood their emotional trauma.

It was into this scene that Talibah entered, nearly breaking the silence with a pronouncement. Instead, she embraced the situation and, crossing the room, put her arms around the young women as a show of her care and concern.

After a few moments, Talibah pulled away and spoke. "Ladies, Aaqil and I will be staying at the dig to continue the work. We not only have an obligation to science, but we have an even deeper obligation to Frank, Sophie, other team members, and the Israeli soldiers, all who have given up so much. This is the best way for us to honor their memory.

As for you, there will be a bus leaving in ten minutes to take you to Ben Gurion Airport in Tel Aviv. From there, you will be flown directly to Amman and should be home later this evening." Talibah had tried to sound upbeat, but the raw emotions that had surfaced for the coeds clouded any enthusiastic response.

'Thank you, Talibah" responded Moriah. "I think the girls will be more appreciative once they have boarded the plane and are on their way home. As for me, I intend to stay here at the dig site and help where I can."

The coeds pulled away with looks of shock on their faces. "You can't do that!" screamed Caroline. "That's insane!" Evelyn put her arm around Carolyn attempting to calm her.

Jameelah turned toward Carolyn. "You don't understand the violence over here because you have lived in the protected cocoon of America. "For us…" waving her arm to include Moriah and Gamila, "…fighting and bloodshed is a way of life. I don't condone it, I wish it wouldn't occur, but I accept it as a fact of life in the Middle East."

Evelyn was the next to speak up. "Okay, I understand that it is a way of life here. But, we don't have to court danger at every turn! Moriah, you have to return with us. We have to know that you will be safe!"

Moriah smiled a mother's knowing smile. "Ladies, this is my home; this is my land. And, while I'm not a soldier or an archaeologist, I can continue to help. I have a *need* to help, even if, for no other reason, than to honor those who have given up so much. Go back to the university . . . better yet, go home. I will send a note to the dean explaining the situation and requesting you be given four weeks of leave from your studies. I'm sure he will concur that there have been extenuating circumstances. Come, let us say good-bye."

The coeds gave Moriah a hug before turning and slowly leaving the tent. After they had left, Talibah walked up to Moriah and spoke softly. "I don't know if you're an Israeli patriot or a glutton for punishment" she smiled.

Moriah returned the smile. "All Israeli's are patriots."

She put her arm around Talibah and the two women exited the tent, turning southwest toward the dig site, now surrounded by military vehicles.

3D.4 Kruglov's Escape

\* \* \* \* \* \* \* \* \* \* \* \* \* \* \* \* \* \* \* \* \* \* \* \* \* \* \* \* \*

Although having been trapped in his underground bunker for two days, Kruglov had not been unduly deprived. He had plenty of food and water, sleeping quarters, a hot shower, and the companionship of his mistress.

But the warrior in him was growing restless. *There had to be a way out of this subterranean prison!* he thought. Something in the back of his mind kept bothering him. He could vaguely recall a briefing about this facility many years ago when cold war bunkers were commonplace - it's sophisticated electronics, the missile batteries, the self-contained utility, the bunker construction, it's variety of access points, food storage and kitchen facilities, . . . .

*That's it! The bunker had multiple access points!*

While the elevator was the primary means for accessing the underground bunker, construction tunnels had been used to keep the prying eyes of U.S. spy satellites from seeing the actual construction occurring underground. While most of the construction tunnels had been backfilled, there was one that had been left open for resupplies and technology upgrades.

The question now was, 'Where was that tunnel entrance'?

"Tanya!" he blurted out. "You must help me find a hidden door in one of these walls. It will allow us to get out of here and back to civilization."

Tanya greeted him with a blank stare, still attempting to get her mind around what had happened two days ago that led them into this tomb. She hesitated too long.

"Tanya! Get off your butt and get moving! The sooner we find this door, the sooner we'll get out of here!"

Tanya rose quickly and began her search. If there was one thing she had learned since becoming Kruglov's mistress several years ago, he was not one to be trifled with.

The bunker was nearly 40,000 square feet in size with multiple rooms. After they had spent nearly thirty minutes in the operations wing looking for trap doors and false walls, Tanya suddenly stopped and turned toward Kruglov.

"What did you say the tunnel was used for?" she asked.

"It was used during construction for excavation, later for building materials and equipment installations, and finally for resupply and technician entrance."

"Well then," she responded, "wouldn't it be near where those services now take place? Like, maybe the kitchen or the mechanical equipment room?"

Kruglov stared at her with a blank expression. He was not use to attractive women being so pragmatic and logical. But, maybe that's why Tanya had stood out to him several years ago – she was different.

"Tanya" he replied, "I am going to buy you an expensive gift when we return to Moscow . . . you've earned it! Come, let's go to the kitchen and see if there is a loading door that is still in use."

With a wave of his hand, they proceeded down a long hallway toward the commissary. Entering a large lunchroom, they walked straight toward the kitchen facility.

"Look for where the freezers are" Tanya stated. "Incoming meat would need to remain cold, so the freezers would need to be near a loading area."

Sure enough, as they approached the kitchen freezers, a large 6' x 8' door appeared around the corner, flanked by several two-wheeled dollies.

Kruglov opened the door to find a loading dock positioned at the end of a long tunnel, 10 meters wide x 8 meters high, that extended off into the distance. Feeling the dark wall surface, he found a light switch that activated hundreds of lights, illuminating the length of the tunnel.

Sighing with relief that he had finally found an exit from their underground prison, Kruglov took Tanya by the hand and began walking off into the distance, not sure where the tunnel's entrance would exit into the countryside.

3D.5 Abducted

\* \* \* \* \* \* \* \* \* \* \* \* \* \* \* \* \* \* \* \* \* \* \* \* \*

As the dig began to start up, emphasis was being placed on two areas. The first was where Frank had been working - the alcove containing wooden shelves and possible ancient scrolls.

The second area was focused on the library's anteroom, on the west side of the library that appeared to contain remnants of the wagon and a possible sarcophagus.

Although uncovering other areas of the site was important for arriving at a complete archaeological record, the shortage of personnel, combined with the proximity of geopolitical danger, necessitated a prioritization occur in regard to work effort.

Soon, the dig site as bustling with activity as if the terrorist attack had never occurred.

Meanwhile, the coeds, Abdul, Hadiya, Michael, Agnes, along with other dig personnel who had elected to leave the danger, were calmly riding the bus making its way back to Tel Aviv and Ben Gurion Airport as the sun began to set below the horizon.

Traveling south along No. 2 Road, the bus had passed the Ya'ar Hadera Forest and was now driving through Mikhmoret. The bus driver had taken this coastal road thinking the scenery would aid in helping the passengers deal with the last several days of trauma. At the southern end of the town, the road curved towards the ocean and eventually place them within 1,000 feet of the gentle water of the Mediterranean Sea.

The bus approached the bridge that spanned the Alexander Stream. Over the centuries, the Stream carved a channel though the landscape and, at its entrance to the Sea, the land was canyon-like and desolate.

As the bus approached the bridge, the setting sun's rays reflected off the Mediterranean's surface, producing a glare on the windshield of the bus, obscuring the driver's view. It also masked the presence of military personnel crouched by the side of the road.

The first explosion destroyed the abutment on the north end of the bridge, the resulting debris striking the bus and stopping it abruptly. The second explosion occurred behind the bus, thus preventing it from backing up and escaping.

Almost instantly, a carefully directed barrage of automatic weapons fire riddled the front of the bus, killing the driver and the two Israeli guards. A small explosive charge was quickly attached to the door and, following a three second pause, detonated, dislocating the door from its hinges.

Members of Iran's IRGC, who had come ashore the prior evening, stormed the bus, binding hostages with plastic ties and covering their heads with dark hoods.

Informants had relayed the news of the departing archaeology personnel to the IRGC, whose mission was to capture hostages in the event they could be used during a negotiation at a later date.

Within three minutes, the bus had been evacuated and the hostages were forced down the embankment and loaded into three off-road vehicles that took them to two speed boats waiting at the mouth of the Alexander Stream. Four minutes later, the two boats had been loaded and were on their way toward the open water of the Mediterranean and a waiting Iranian submarine that had quietly entered the Sea during the dark hours of the prior evening.

Within ten minutes of the first explosion, police from nearby Mikhmoret and Netanya had converged on the bridge, but aside from the destruction and bullet-riddle bus, there was no one to be found. And, while they scouted the area for anyone connected dig site, they did not hear the two Iranian boats motoring off into the darkness.

Within thirty minutes, news of the abduction had reached Israeli military command. Units were dispatched to scour the countryside but, with no definitive information as to which terrorist organization had executed the abduction, it was like finding a needle in a haystack. No one suspected the Iranians would have had a direct hand in this event nor a secret submarine in the Mediterranean.

Fifteen minutes later, Colonel Beagan received a phone call at his outpost at the Nahsholim dig site alerting him to the abduction. Amid the flurry of angry exchanges, he learned that there were no leads in the disappearance of the civilian dig volunteers. He slammed down the phone receiver and paced his tent. When his anger had finally cooled, he left his tent in search of the EMA and IMA Directors.

They would not be happy about this.

3D.6 London

\* \* \* \* \* \* \* \* \* \* \* \* \* \* \* \* \* \* \* \* \* \* \* \* \* \* \*

Like a strobe light capturing static motion, the brilliance of the RVB detonation at 9:00am froze images of life at Bank Station near the heart of London's financial district.

*IWO* operatives had smuggled the RVB into Great Britain in a small fishing boat that crossed the Channel between Calais and Folkstone. Here, it was stored in the garage of a local house that had been rented several months earlier.

After receiving instructions on the date and time for the detonation, a small panel truck labeled with the name of a fictitious plumbing company was used by the operatives to transport the RVB to Croydon. The bomb was then transferred to a grocery delivery truck for the final twenty-kilometer journey to Bank Station. Once in place, the operatives loaded two carts with fresh produce, maintaining their ruse as they made their way to various restaurants, eventually disappearing into the crowd.

Unlike an air burst that maximized the design effectiveness of an RVB detonation, the London RVB's location in the back of the delivery truck necessitated a ground burst. While resulting in a sizeable crater, the damaging effects of the weapon were mitigated by the proximity of nearby buildings.

Nonetheless, the effects of the blast were devastating. People within 100 meters line-of-sight of the truck were vaporized in the initial fireball. Those within 200 meters were instantly killed by the explosion's shock wave. Many others succumbed to falling debris as older, less stable buildings crumbled in the face of the overwhelming physics of the bomb.

Dust choked the air and, for a period of fifteen minutes, daylight turned to dusk. As the cloud of debris slowly settled back to earth, four square blocks London's popular financial district took on the appearance of London during the blitz in World War II. Fires raged in many buildings, having been set ablaze by the RVB's thermal design.

In the distance, loose pieces of buildings continued to fall to the ground with an occasional crackle and thud. The numerous fires combined in a cacophony that resembled the roar of a passing thunderstorm. Those who had made it to safety were afraid to enter the streets for fear of a follow-on attack. Those who remained on the streets – those still alive – suffered from injuries, shock, and a loss of hearing due to the enormity of the blast.

At what seemed like hours, only minutes past as emergency responders began to arrive, making their way through the cataclysm of wreckage and death.

## 3D.7 Brasilia

\* \* \* \* \* \* \* \* \* \* \* \* \* \* \* \* \* \* \* \* \* \* \* \* \* \* \*

The Fairchild C-119 aircraft had seen better days. Nicknamed the "Flying Boxcar" because of its ability to haul enormous amounts of cargo, it had been built in 1952 and, after more than 65 years of service, was barely air worthy.

Nonetheless, the two *IWO* agents bought the aircraft from a regional freight hauler and had reconfigured the aircraft. All non-essential equipment and electronics had been removed to increase the aircraft's cargo take-off weight, necessary to enable them to carry one item . . . a Russian made vacuum bomb.

As they preflighted the aircraft at a secluded section of the Brasília–Presidente Juscelino Kubitschek International Airport, the agents' anxiety level began to rise. Fear of discovery or the resulting wrath of Aarzam made them complete their tasks quickly and efficiently. Too much of *IWO's* plan was riding on their mission's success . . . they couldn't let their leader down.

Now seated in the cockpit, they completed their checklist and started the engines. The two large two R-4360-30 radial engines chugged to life, belching smoke and backfiring before arriving at a dull operating rhythm. The only instruments in the panel consisted of a compass, an altimeter, a small handheld transceiver, and a portable GPS.

After requesting taxi clearance, they positioned the old aircraft for take-off on runway 29L which would have them taking off to the west. After departure, they would make a right turn north to the city of Brasilia only ten miles away.

Normally requiring 2,300 feet of runway for takeoff, the weight of the RVB strained the C-119's two old engines from producing the speed as they once were designed. Nonetheless, they lumbered down the runway slowly, but steadily, gaining speed.

In the control tower, the controllers watched the aircraft pass its normal takeoff point and began debating why the aircraft was not taking off.

"C-119 QXBR, Brasilia Tower. Are you having difficulty? Do you want to abort your takeoff?"

The agents looked at one another in shock. They were not expecting to be challenged by anyone.

Haltingly, the pilot responded. "This is C-119 QXBR. Negative, we are continuing our takeoff roll. Hauling extra supplies today, so the load is a little heavier than normal."

"Roger" replied the controller. "Safe travels. After departure, climb right to 2,000 feet and proceed on course."

"Roger, climb right to 2,000 feet and proceed on course. C-119 QXBR out." The agents smiled at one another. Their brief flight training had paid off, allowing them to learn how to speak correctly to airport controllers without raising suspicion.

As the end of the 10,000-foot runway came into view, the old aircraft finally reached its takeoff speed of 110 knots. Slowly, the pilot coaxed the front wheel off the ground and, after what seemed like an eternity, the mains left the runway with five hundred feet to spare.

Watching from the control tower, the two controllers shook their head in amazement, amazed how close the plane had come to running off the end of the runway.

The plane made a slow turn to the right, heading northeast toward the city of Brasilia. At 140 knots, the travel time to their detonation point would only take four minutes. Both began to repeat their rehearsed prayer.

*"Wa jaalna mim baina aideehim saddan wa min khlfahum saddan fa aghshainahum fahum la ubsaroon."* ("And we have put a barrier before them, and a barrier behind them, and we have covered them up, so that they cannot see.")[6]

Ground zero for the RVB's detonation was the Cathedral of Brasilia. Easy to spot from the air, the 32,000 square foot Roman Catholic Cathedral was known for its architectural design of incorporating sixteen curved concrete columns providing exoskeletal support to the structure.

As the plane dropped to 1,000 feet in altitude during the last minute of flight, the two agents ignored frantic calls from Brasilia's tower controllers who were viewing the rapid change in altitude on their radar display in the control tower. The two agents smiled at one another as the copilot toggled the detonation switch on the control yoke.

At 9:00am local time, the brilliance of the thermobaric air burst from the RVB lit up the Brasilia sky like a hundred suns. Although the same type of RVB that exploded in London, the aircraft delivery of the Brasilia RVB permitted an air burst to occur, the most advantageous method for delivering the maximum destructive power of an RVB.

When the fuel-air mixture ignited, the resulting fireball engulfed three square blocks of the city. Immediately following the initial pressure wave was the resulting rarefaction (vacuum) that killed people by rupturing their lungs.[7]

In the blink of an eye, those within 1,000 feet of ground zero were killed. Those directly exposed to the blast's fireball were vaporized. Weakened buildings collapsed, killing those within who had managed to escape the initial explosion.

After thirty minutes, the dust began to settle. Life seemed to stop in Brasilia that morning, both literally and figuratively. In what was a teaming metropolis, over 7,000 people ceased to exist.

Within another thirty minutes, news stations began to broadcast from the destruction, competing with London's own bombing news, that the same tragedy occurred in their hometown of Brasilia.

While the world was shocked once again, the news was joyously received in Aarzam's headquarters. Shouts and jubilation of yet another successful RVB detonation, along with a high death toll, buoyed *IWO* members' spirits and reinforced their divine interpretation of their cause.

Aarzam could barely contain his excitement. He had successfully initiated five "cuts" (attacks) on the Western Alliance without any reprisals. And, while the Western Alliance had begun to counter-attack, Aarzam felt comfortable that he had them back on their heels. With the unexpected and widely distributed attacks nature of IWO's attacks, the Western Alliance would be unable to mount an effective offense. Now, with IWO using RVB's as part of their assault, conceived as part of Abbas' original battle strategy, the West's response would be further diluted as they rendered aid to these mass-casualty events.

Aarzam smiled as he slowly swiveled in his chair to gaze out the window at a vast landscape. His mind began to wander at the possibility of winning this conflict and becoming the Supreme Ruler.

## 3D.8 Emergence

\* \* \* \* \* \* \* \* \* \* \* \* \* \* \* \* \* \* \* \* \* \* \* \* \*

As soon as Kruglov and Tanya emerged from the tunnel, they found themselves 2,000 meters north of Kruglov's former remote headquarter buildings that had been destroyed in the Iranian air attack. Finding themselves within one mile of the Tbilisi International Airport's main terminal, Kruglov and Tanya began walking toward the airport manager's office located on the second floor.

Upon arriving thirty minutes later, the manager was greatly surprised to see Kruglov walk through his office door. While normally the final authority at the airport, the manager quickly deferred to the famous general standing before him.

"I need the use of your office!" bellowed Kruglov. "Go away!"

With a shocked look on his face, the manager knew better than to question someone of Kruglov's position and quickly departed the room, closing the door behind him.

Kruglov felt 'out-of-the-know'. He had to get in touch with Arthur and Pao to see what other mischief *IWO* was causing.

\*\*\*\*\*\*\*\*\*\*\*\*\*\*\*\*\*\*\*\*\*\*\*\*\*\*\*\*\*\*\*\*\*\*\*\*\*\*\*\*\*\*

Under Pao's direction, Chin had compiled a list of personnel who had been previously identified as double agents. While China had successfully used double agents in the past, recent attacks on Kruglov's and Pao's field headquarters made their continued use problematic.

Marching into Pao's office, Chin snapped to attention and handed the report to Pao.

"Here is the list of double agents that we have used in the past" stated Chin.

Without perusing the list, Pao let the papers fall to his desk. "Get rid of all of them . . . today!" he said firmly.

Chin rendered a quick salute, wheeling about and exited Pao's office. Within a few minutes, Pao could here Chin issuing orders to Pao's "special troops" to execute Pao's directive against the double agents. It made no difference in which country the double agents were located. By the end of the day, they would all be dead.

After Chin's departure from his office, Pao began to think of Arthur. With Kruglov apparently out of the picture, they needed to talk.

✳✳✳✳✳✳✳✳✳✳✳✳✳✳✳✳✳✳✳✳✳✳✳✳✳✳✳✳✳✳✳✳✳✳✳✳✳✳✳✳✳✳✳✳

Arthur was receiving updates on the progression of *IWO*'s coordinated attacks on Western Alliance interests through his backchannels comprised of senior military personnel. In addition, Colonel Butterman had resurfaced and, having made his way to Arthur's location at the small airstrip located just north of the coastal town of Bahia de los Angeles in Baja California, was coordinating all incoming field intelligence.

Although *IWO* was Arthur's sworn enemy, he had to admire the completeness of what had to have been Abbas' strategic plan in prosecuting multiple targets in rapid-fire succession, effectively diluting Western Alliance forces and catching them off-guard. While confident that Aarzam was now the operational authority for *IWO*, Arthur still held out faith of Abbas' true intention of wanting to avoid a conflict whose only result would be mutually assured destruction.

Unfortunately, he had no information to know whether Abbas had regained control of *IWO* and was conducting these attacks himself. Conversely, he also did not know if Abbas was still alive, having become a victim of Aarzam's thirst for glory.

He just didn't know.

Nonetheless, Arthur had been busying himself with planning and executing conventional weapons strikes against *IWO* targets in an attempt to interrupt their global initiative. By maintaining control of a number of the strategic forces, due to the loyalty of his field commanders, Arthur was modifying Clancy's operational directives in order to ensure proportional force responses were being executed. Such was the case in yesterday's aerial attack on *IWO* training and logistics centers housing ordnance and ammunition yet to be distributed to *IWO* forces. These aerial bombings had crippled *IWO*'s ability to supply their terrorist forces with much-needed ammunition and weaponry.

In the abandoned hangar, Butterman burst into Arthur's office. "Arthur, you've got to see this!"

Butterman laid his laptop on Arthur's desk, now showing streaming video of the RVB attacks in London and Brasilia.

"What do we know?" asked Arthur.

Butterman continued. "News reports are reporting unofficial military assessments indicating *IWO* is using RVB's. It's the only thing that could cause that level of damage without being nuclear."

"Well, it looks like Kruglov's stolen RVB's have surfaced." Arthur mused, shaking his head slowly as he viewed the streaming video. "Damn, I wish he would have had those things secured."

"How do we respond to this escalation?" inquired Butterman.

Arthur sighed. He never wanted to use nuclear weapons in the conflict with *IWO*. If he did, it would mean traveling along a path of no return.

Arthur looked up at Butterman.

"We're going to continue using conventional weapons, but we're going to increase the pace of missions. I want sorties scheduled seven days per week, twenty-four hours per day. We're not going to let *IWO* breathe.

Let's look at *IWO's* global tactical locations and divide them into regions that complement our distribution of aviation and missile resources. Our new ROE (Rules of Engagement) will essentially create a free-fire zone in each tactical theater. I want this new protocol initiated in two hours. Let's get the word out."

Butterman nodded and wheeled around out of the office. Within one minute, he was arranging a conference call with all of Arthur's loyal commanders to inform them of the new ROE. He knew that the commanders would appreciate this type of ROE – it was simple, easy to understand, and allowed them to exercise their creativity in executing new battle orders.

Fifteen minutes later, he hung up the phone. Mission accomplished.

3D.9 Atlanta

\* \* \* \* \* \* \* \* \* \* \* \* \* \* \* \* \* \* \* \* \* \* \* \* \* \* \*

The two *IWO* agents had made their way into the U.S. through the southern border separating the U.S. from Mexico. They had hired a private "coyote" (guide for hire) to take them from Mexico City north to a porous section of the border adjacent to Big Bend National Park, Texas.  Just prior to crossing the border, they killed the coyote to ensure their presence would remain unknown.

They crossed the river and made their way to Cottonwood, Texas near the Castolon campground.  The campground was closed due to recent wildfires, making it the perfect place for a Winnebago motor home, hidden by their co-conspirators a week earlier.

The two agents had five days to make the 1,400-mile journey to Atlanta.  The Winnebago, stocked with food and essential supplies, afforded them the ability to travel incognito, with the exception of the occasional fuel stop.

Three days later, they pulled into an RV park near Tallapoosa, Georgia, approximately 60 miles from Hartsfield-Jackson Atlanta International Airport - ground zero for their RVB.

The RVB they would be detonating had been shipped separately.  Transported from the Middle East, it arrived via an old, non-descript freighter in the Port of Tampico, Mexico. From there, it was transferred to a fishing trawler that subsequently tracked the coastline northward to the fishing docks located at Mobile Bay, Alabama.

Once in the harbor, the trawler blended in with many other vessels, becoming just one more fishing boat among hundreds. Mooring at a remote end of the dock, the *IWO* crew used a rented hoist to lift the camouflaged RVB off the deck of the trawler and into the trailer of a rented commercial truck.

These *IWO* agents then proceeded north along U.S. Highway 65 to Montgomery, Alabama. From there, they changed to U.S. Highway 85 to Hartsfield-Jackson Atlanta International Airport, parking in a commercial trailer lot near the airport. The entire trip from Mobile took less than five hours.

Renting a car, this second *IWO* team traveled to the RV park near Tallapoosa, Georgia to join their comrades and celebrate the impending culmination of months of preparation. With the attack set for the following morning, the level of excitement and anticipation was palpable.

Early the next morning, the four agents arose and traveled to the commercial truck lot near the Atlanta airport. They left the Winnebago at the RV park to avoid attracting attention in the city.

Once at the commercial parking lot, two of the agents checked the truck and trailer while the other two prepared the wiring and detonation circuitry for the RVB. Testing the circuitry with a small flashbulb, they all cheered when the bulb brilliantly illuminated for a fraction of a second indicating a functioning detonation circuit. The wires were then switched from the bulb to the RVB's detonator.

The plan was for the rental car and the tractor trailer truck to drive through the nearby airport property fence and proceed toward the area between Concourse A and Concourse T, the main domestic terminal. The car would be in front of the truck, prepared to ram any security vehicles attempting to stop the truck. Once they penetrated the airport property fence, they would need only two minutes to reach their target.

At 8:50am, they started their engines and proceeded north along the east side of the airport property on Loop Road. At the traffic light with the M.H. Jackson Service Road, they turned left toward the airport. Nearing the location of the Control tower, the road bent to the right at a security checkpoint. Beyond that were two more security gates.

As they approached the checkpoint, the passenger in the rental car tightened the silencer on his pistol. Upon slowing to a stop, the guard approached to check their identification credentials. He was just about to make the request when the pistol's muffled "poof poof" discharge resulted in the guard collapsing next to the car.

Both vehicles now made their way to the remaining security gates at which there were no security personnel. The truck now took the lead in order to use its weight and inertia to ram through the two remaining gates.

The first gate exploded off the front grill of the truck, flying off to the right and hitting an adjacent building. They had to slow to make a sharp left turn and then through the last security gate. Once it was down, the rental car retook the lead and both accelerated across along Taxiway "F" next to Runway 26 Left.

By now, the Airport Police had been alerted to the earlier gate crashing. They, in turn, notified the Control Tower of the security intrusion.

As the Tower Controller looked up from the phone, he caught sight of the two vehicles increasing their speed along the Taxiway "F". I've got them in sight!" he shouted into the phone. "They are westbound on Taxiway "F" at a high rate of speed! Heading toward the concourses!"

As they sped along, the *IWO* agents looked to their right with blank expressions at the numerous airliners lined up on Taxiway "E", heading for departure.

They passed the north side of Concourse A and turned left onto Ramp 1. Straight ahead was Concourse T, the Domestic Main Terminal.

The truck driver looked at his watch. It had been just under two minutes since they shot the security guard. *'Right on time'* he thought.

The truck wove between the departing and parked aircraft to head toward the main ramp entry to Concourse T. Seeing that the truck would make it to its destination, the two agents in the rental car made the last minute decision to ram the nearest fuel truck, currently refueling a large Airbus A380 airliner.

In the tractor trailer, the explosion of the fuel truck was reflected in the rear-view mirrors as a brilliant white light. The two agents looked at one another and smiled, knowing they were going to be successful in their mission.

Three seconds later, they achieved success and the martyrdom they longed for.

In the Control Tower, the controllers were just starting to announce an emergency declaration to aircraft on the ground and in the air when the fuel tanker exploded, the fireball arching over the top of Terminal A. They paused long enough to witness the subsequent detonation of the RVB.

Then, they were gone.

3D.10 The War Comes Home

\* \* \* \* \* \* \* \* \* \* \* \* \* \* \* \* \* \* \* \* \* \* \* \* \* \*

Although the ground burst in Atlanta was not optimal for an RVB, the proximity of other aircraft and fuel trucks on Ramp 1 only served to add to the devastation of the RVB explosion. One by one, in rapid succession, aircraft began to explode, falling victim to the jet fuel ignited within their wings.

The RVB detonated on Ramp 1 between Concourses T and A. Concourse T had seventeen gates facing the ramp while Concourse A had thirteen. There were aircraft at every gate and several on the ramp making their way out to Taxiway F for departure. The five thousand people aboard those aircraft disappeared.

The initial pressure wave of the blast shattered the terminal glass windows, cutting down those within. Then came the 2,200°F fireball that crept into every room and hallway, consuming both terminals. Finally, the subsequent rarefaction killed people by rupturing their lungs as the air rushed back in to fill the void caused by the pressure wave.

Ten thousand people vanished and countless thousands more were injured.

*IWO* had succeeded once again and, this time, on American soil.

## 3D.11 Finding the Needle

\* \* \* \* \* \* \* \* \* \* \* \* \* \* \* \* \* \* \* \* \* \* \* \* \* \* \*

Arthur was now on his laptop, attempting to analyze the London and Brasilia bombings for any similarities or clues. He made a list of what he knew.

- *Kruglov lost 25 RVB's to IWO.*
- *IWO seems to be targeting capital cities or, at least, large cities where there will be a maximum probability of casualties.*
- *Both bombings occurred near 9:00am local time, when the municipal centers would be the most crowded.*
- *The London bombing was a ground burst.*
- *The Brasilia bombing was an air burst.*
- *The second bombing was west of the first – could IWO be detonating RVB's according to time zones?*

Arthur knew that he needed to anticipate where future bombings would occur. He had to make an attempt to interrupt any plans for detonation despite having no knowledge of where the next targets would be or how the detonations would occur.

It was like trying to find a needle in a haystack.

His only option was to make up a list of potential target cities and then notify each mayor of a potential impending threat. But how could he do that? There were hundreds of large cities in the Western Alliance.

He continued to review his list of known observations. After some time, he decided to focus capital cities and selected mega-cities in each time zone. While still comprising a large list, it helped him to narrow his focus within each time zone. And, knowing that *IWO* only had twenty-five RVB's, they also would be limited in what they could have included in their targeting plan. This would mean essentially one RVB for every world time zone with one left over in reserve.

After about an hour, Arthur felt comfortable with the list he had created. It was a long shot that it might be useful, but at least city mayors would have foreknowledge of an imminent threat even if he couldn't confirm the existence of a specific target. Maybe the advanced warning would enable them to put their emergency plans into place for a quicker response should one be needed.

He could only hope.

It was now 7:00am. The sun had crested the horizon an hour ago and light was now flooding into the partially hangar door.

Arthur had just stood up to give his notification list to Butterman when the colonel burst through the door, a dreaded look on his face.

"They got Atlanta!" he stammered.

Arthur looked at his watch.

It was 9:07am in Atlanta.

## 3D.12 Regret

\* \* \* \* \* \* \* \* \* \* \* \* \* \* \* \* \* \* \* \* \* \* \* \* \* \* \*

Putting together reports from airline pilots, emergency personnel, and news outlets, Butterman was able to piece together an overview of the devastation that occurred in Atlanta.

As he began his briefing at 7:30am local time, Arthur and the rest of the Challenger 650 flight crew sat in stunned silence. The pictures streaming over the Internet depicted a catastrophic event.

When Butterman concluded his briefing, Arthur rose from his chair and quietly walked outside to be alone with his thoughts. All he could think about was how close he and Abbas had come to averting this conflict. How he had been too lax with Clancy, letting the latter exercise too much control over military forces. How he should have responded quicker and with much more aggressive tactics to overcome *IWO's* efforts.

After a few minutes, he turned toward the hangar only to see the rest of the team watching him. He quickened his pace and, upon reaching the door, looked at Jefferson and declared "Let's gear up! I want to be able to leave within the hour." The pilot gave a 'thumbs-up', signaled to the co-pilot and began his preflight safety checks on the Challenger 650.

Arthur continued. "Butterman, let's get this potential target list out to the mayors of the cities I have listed. Atlanta was on my list but, unfortunately, I'm not sure how much good it would have been to notify them in advance of the bomb since we didn't have any information on where it would have been placed within the city."

Got it!" replied Butterman.

"And get Smythe and Torrey on the line. I want to see how we can increase our assault performance."

"Roger that!" replied Butterman.

It was time to get back into the game.

## 3D.13 Reaching Out

\* \* \* \* \* \* \* \* \* \* \* \* \* \* \* \* \* \* \* \* \* \* \* \* \* \*

Abbas finally made it to a safe house after the missile attack in the village of Harjiwan. He decided to stay at his personal residence only briefly as he felt it would be under surveillance by Aarzam loyalists.

For the first couple of days, he had felt unsteady on his feet due to a concussion he assumed he sustained from the explosions at the cafe. But, even though he was light-headed at times, he still wore a shoulder holster carrying a 9mm Beretta pistol as protection from unexpected guests.

He was receiving reports from his network of supporters on the emerging conflict with the Western Alliance. He shook his head at the thought that Arthur, Kruglov, Pao, and he were such great leaders; yet, all made fatal strategic mistakes with respect to the forces they individually commanded, principally an over-reliance on 'trusted' subordinates.

Abbas also thought of what Arthur must be thinking at this point in time. Aarzam had been faithfully executing *IWO's* strategic battle plan flawlessly. Arthur would have recognized Abbas as the author of that plan and would be wondering if Abbas had reneged on the peace commitments he had previously represented to Arthur.

*Would Arthur trust him enough to receive a personal phone call? Was the West so committed to its air campaign against*

*IWO that it couldn't be stopped? Was there still an opportunity to bring this conflict to a peaceful resolution, or was it too late?*

There was only one way to find out. He had to call Arthur. As he picked up the phone, the sound of footsteps outside the closed window drew his attention. He slowly placed the phone on a nearby table and moved to the corner of the room. Crouching down behind a chair, he drew his pistol and took aim at the nearby door.

He watched the handle slowly turn on the door he had carefully locked earlier. As the door gradually opened, he cocked the hammer on the pistol.

The figure crept into the room cautiously as if to know that there was imminent danger ahead. Recognizing there was no way to enter unaware, the figure let out a sigh and declared "Abbas, it's me! Don't shoot!"

Rasha entered the house backwards with her hands up, not knowing where Abbas had secreted himself. She made sure her long black hair was visible outside her tunic so that there would be no mistaking her for a woman.

Abbas relaxed his grip on the pistol and stood up. "You almost went to Valhalla, little one."

"Valhalla? Where's that?" she asked.

Abbas smiled. "It's a mythical land, the final resting place for Viking warriors to commune with their gods."

Rasha smiled in acknowledgment. "I could see myself alone with a bunch of Viking warriors" she retorted as she smiled and cast a flirtatious glance at Abbas.

Abbas just shook his head. While he appreciated Rasha's attempt at light-heartedness, the global conflict consumed his thoughts.

"I must get ahold of Arthur. Can you stand watch?"

She pulled an AK-47 rifle from under her tunic. "No problem."

From the reports Abbas had received, the Western Alliance was in increasing their level of retaliation, launching continuous air strikes and missile attacks against *IWO* assets.

Given the sequencing of *IWO's* attacks – ships, naval assets, car and electronic bombs . . . Abbas assessed that Aarzam was either on the verge of executing the scheduled detonation of RVB's or had already begun those attacks. If so, he couldn't imagine anything that would push Arthur closer toward the retaliatory use of nuclear weapons than RVB attacks on Western Alliance population centers.

Abbas' strategic battle plan had been too good. It was so precise and devastating in its effects that it left no room for retreat or repeal. His purpose in its creation was to develop a deterrent so massive in its potential impact as to force peace talks with, and concessions from, the West. He had never intended to place it into operation.

With a final sigh, he looked at Rasha. She was staring at him from across the room as he picked up the phone and dialed Arthur's number.

He had to stop this conflict.

## 3D.14 Unexpected Calls

\* \* \* \* \* \* \* \* \* \* \* \* \* \* \* \* \* \* \* \* \* \* \* \* \* \*

Arthur's phone rang. He glanced at the caller ID – he didn't recognize the number, but it was Russian.

"Yes?" Arthur answered tentatively.

"What the hell is going on?! the other voice said loudly. My base gets blown up, there are explosions in cities everywhere, and I'm hearing of RVB's are being detonated! What the hell are you doing about it?!"

It was Kruglov.

"It's about time you called." Arthur responded. "While you have been on 'vacation', the world has gone to crazy."

"Vacation?!" Kruglov chuckled. "Boy, the stories I could tell you."

As Arthur was about to respond, his phone signaled an incoming call.

It was Pao.

"Kruglov, hold on. Pao is calling on the other line. I'm going to patch him in."

"Pao, good afternoon. I've got you conferenced in with Kruglov."

Pao began. "Gentlemen, I did not know if we would ever have the opportunity to speak with one another again. It seems we have all been sharing in the same bad luck the last few days. I knew of the attempt Arthur's life and was surprised to hear of your misfortune, Kruglov. It is good that you're okay."

"And, I hear that you received a visit from the same Mig's that visited me" Kruglov responded, referring to the attack on Pao's headquarters in Hotan.

"Yes, but they will not be doing any more visiting. We shot them down." Pao said dryly. "However, I would like to hear of your adventures at another time."

"So would I" interrupted Arthur. "But, right now, we have some strategizing to do. *IWO* has reached what I believe to be the final phase in their offensive . . . the use of Kruglov's RVB's."

On the other end of the phone. Kruglov winced at the mention of the weapons that were stolen from his armories.

Arthur continued. "From my analysis, *IWO* appears to be targeting major population centers in successive time zones. All of the attacks have occurred at or near 9:00am local time. London and Atlanta were ground detonations but the one in Brasilia was an aerial burst. I thought there would be more targeted explosions in the U.S. following Atlanta, but there haven't been any. The next several 9:00am time zones occur in the Pacific Ocean, which means the next major land mass with large populations is the Orient – Japan and China. I sent out a list of possible targets to city mayors, but, short of knowing precisely where the bombs will explode, my list may be nothing more than an advanced warning."

Pao chimed in. "Abbas' battle plan seems to have called for iterative offensive actions that are individually devastating but, when combined with the successive destruction of naval ships, car bombs, and electronic bombs, the aggregate of the attacks are magnified in terms of collective destruction. In addition, those were not one-time attacks. Car bombs and electronic bombs are continuing to occur and I am sure we'll see more naval ship attacks."

"What are you saying?" inquired Kruglov.

Pao responded. "I'm saying that I doubt Abbas would detonate all of his RVB's in one fell swoop. Rather, he would space them out as he has the other attacks. The longer he can keep up these types of assaults, the greater the need to dilute our own forces to respond to these attacks. If he has twenty-five RVB's, I would only see him using six to eight of them in one offensive cycle. The rest will be kept for a future, multiple attack sequences."

"An excellent assessment" added Arthur. "But, even if he limits his current assault to six to eight RVB's, that means there are still three to five cities remaining that are currently being targeted."

Pao interrupted. "While Tokyo would be the only obvious target in Japan, China has many more high population centers.

Shanghai, Beijing, Guangzhou, Shenzhen, and Tianjin all have populations in excess of ten million people."

True, and we can't forget about other major cities as we proceed westward such as Singapore, although smaller than the cities you mention in China, is a major financial center" added Kruglov.

"I will focus my efforts on securing our five largest cities" Pao stated. "Since aviation is so restricted in China, I will assume a possible ground attack and will deploy military troops accordingly. Through surveillance and the standing-up of numerous checkpoints, we might be able to avert disaster."

Kruglov," stated Arthur "in addition to monitoring Moscow, you may want to also surveil smaller cities that have cultural or strategic significance. I sense that one of the intents of Abbas' battle plan is to negatively impact the psyche of the populations he attacks as much as the physical destruction."

"Sounds reasonable" Kruglov responded. "Oh, how I would like to get my hands on Abbas! His *IWO* has caused a great deal of headaches, death, and destruction!

"I don't know if he is even alive" responded Arthur.

"What do you mean?!" shouted Kruglov. "Look at all of the destruction that's taking place!"

"Our intelligence sources reveal that Abbas' own people were trying to kill him before the *IWO* attacks began" responded

Arthur. "In my opinion, what you have been witnessing over the last few days is Aarzam expertly carrying out Abbas' battle plan . . . to perfection. I still hold onto the hope that Abbas never wanted this conflict to occur but, rather, he was a victim of his own subordinates, the same as we were."

While Kruglov and Pao took a moment to reflect on Arthur's observation, his phone signaled an incoming call.

It was Abbas.

### 3D.15 Premature Understanding

\* \* \* \* \* \* \* \* \* \* \* \* \* \* \* \* \* \* \* \* \* \* \* \* \* \*

At first Arthur was stunned. A great deal of time had passed since his last conversation with Abbas. And, while his current focus was on coordinating Western Alliance counterstrikes against *IWO*, he felt compelled to accept the call.

Turning his attention to Pao and Kruglov, he stated "Gentlemen, Abbas is calling in the other line. Let me patch him in."

"Oh, this ought to be good!" Kruglov responded in an aggravated voice.

There were several clicks and then Arthur spoke up. "Abbas, I wasn't expecting your call."

Unaware that he was on a conference line with Pao and Kruglov, Abbas softly responded "My friend, I wasn't sure you would even take my call given all that has happened in the last few days."

Arthur responded with noticeable irritation in his voice. "There have been a lot of people killed since you and I last spoke . . . a lot of needless deaths! I was under the impression you wanted to avoid conflict in favor of working out a peaceful co-existence! What am I to make of all of this?!"

"If I were you,' Abbas began, "I would assume that I had been double-crossed so my opponent would catch me 'flat-footed' and have the momentum on his side when the conflict began."

Abbas' forthrightness took Arthur aback. Abbas wasn't trying to deny his involvement; rather, he was identifying with the Western Alliance.

"You have my attention" Arthur finally responded in a quieter tone. Pao and Kruglov continued to listen quietly in the background.

Abbas began. "I regret not having contacted you sooner. However, I was recovering from a drone strike the Western Alliance launched against my home village of Harjiwan. I was injured in the strike and am still recovering. But it wasn't until I received reports of *IWO* commencing military operations prior to that air strike that I understood why my village was targeted."

He continued. "I thought of the meetings we had, the progress made between us, and the progress we individually achieved with those within our own spheres of influence."

Arthur spoke up. "If I am to believe you, then it would mean that Aarzam is in control of *IWO* and implementing your combat operations plan. Is that true?"

"You are correct. In addition to me, it has come to my attention that attacks have also been conducted against two of my senior personnel, one of which was successful. While I am aware of the Western Alliance's superior surveillance capabilities, the probability of targeted attacks against three of the top four leaders of *IWO* occurring at the same time seems unlikely. Rather, it points to the possibility of an internal coup occurring within *IWO*. I am currently taking actions to regain control and bring *IWO's* offensive to a conclusion."

Arthur wasn't sure how to proceed. Abbas was very convincing and reminded him of the sincerity of their prior conversations.

He decided to respond by introducing Pao and Kruglov into the conversation. "Abbas, when you called, I was in the middle of a conference call with Pao and Kruglov. They are on the line as we speak."

Abbas was taken aback. He thought he had been in a private conversation with Arthur. "Arthur, I . . ."

Before he could continue, Kruglov broke in. "What the hell is the matter with you?!" Still angry at having his forward operating base destroyed while he was in residence, he could not control his temper. "How many thousands of people have died because of your reckless disregard for human life?! Your people even came after me! What the hell is the matter with you?!"

A pause ensued and, albeit no more than a few seconds, was awkward nonetheless.

Abbas broke the silence. "As proof of my desire for peaceful coexistence with the West, let me provide you with the next two planned RVB detonation locations. The first location is Beijing, specifically the 'Monument to the People's Heroes' in Tiananmen Square. One hour later, an explosion is scheduled for the Buddha Tooth Relic Temple in Singapore. Both are targeted for 9:00am local time. Unfortunately, while these are the targets I had originally conceived, I do not know if Aarzam has made any tactical changes in targets."

Arthur chimed in. "So far, we have witnessed detonations in London, Brasilia, and Atlanta."

Abbas responded with notable sadness in his voice. "I . . . I am sorry to hear that. But, it tells me that Aarzam is following the plan as written. Accordingly, I have high confidence regarding the two targets I just spoke of."

Pao spoke up. "Abbas, that's only three hours from now for the Beijing target. If I am to intercede to prevent your agents from detonating RVB's in Beijing and Singapore, I need more information. Telling me the final targets does not help me prevent the placement and detonation of these devices."

Abbas replied. "I am texting their identities, location, and their vehicle description to Arthur's phone, as we speak. Arthur, I need you to forward the message to Pao so he can take action." Abbas knew it was imperative to provide a show of 'good faith' in addressing Pao's concern in order to change the direction of the conflict.

Arthur spoke. "While I am waiting for the text message to arrive, I would like to take advantage of the fact that we are all on the phone together. I know tempers are running high, but we need to maintain level heads in order to resolve the crisis we now find ourselves in."

He continued. "Abbas, it is imperative that we see verifiable action by *IWO* before the Western Alliance will consider ratcheting down its offensive posture. If your information regarding Beijing and Singapore proves useful in preventing any more devastation, then that will be a good first step. But we'll need to see more, such as the winding down and cessation hostilities against Western Alliance targets."

Arthur concluded. "Pao, I just received Abbas' text message. I am forwarding it to you right now."

Kruglov felt the need to speak up. "What about other targets? We know you have twenty-five RVB's. Three have been detonated and two others have just been identified. What are the other twenty targets? WE HAVE TO STOP EVERY ONE OF THOSE before I'll agree to any reduction in my efforts to destroy *IWO*!"

Pao interjected. "Arthur, I have your text message and it's being distributed as we speak."

Turning his attention to Abbas, Pao continued. "Abbas, I am torn between admiring the thoroughness and effectiveness of your offensive strategy, and a deep desire to exterminate all Muslims who support *IWO*. We cannot ignore the suffering that has resulted from the execution of your battle plans by your *IWO* staff. There needs to be a reckoning when this is over. Just as there were war crime trials in Nuremberg at the conclusion of World War II, I will insist the same occur to try members of *IWO* that carried out the bombings over the last few days. We cannot let this stand now or in the future. Even you may not escape prosecution."

While the indignation coming from the Western Alliance leaders was understandable, Abbas was still surprised. While he had been expecting a tense but productive phone call with Arthur, the inclusion of Pao and Kruglov had changed the entire tone of the conversation. *He was trying to forge a path for peace and they were talking of war crimes trials . . . even after he had given them the details of the Beijing and Singapore bombing plans. Had he miscalculated his goodwill gesture in reaching out to Arthur?*

Arthur noticed the silence on Abbas' end of the phone and decided to speak up so as not to lose even a slim opportunity to create a cessation in hostilities.

"Abbas, I appreciate your providing the information to Pao relating to Beijing and Singapore. But, we won't be able to ascertain the value of that information unless, or until, Pao is able to neutralize your agents prior to any detonations.

And, Kruglov brings up a good point. While we might be able to neutralize the next two scheduled bombings, there are still more RVB targets out there that could result in a serious escalation in this conflict . . .not to mention the naval and car bomb attacks that are still occurring.

Here is what I propose. Provide us with detailed information on the remaining twenty RVB targets and begin the process of ceasing all naval and ground attacks. Then, if Pao and Kruglov are able to successfully diffuse the situations in their countries, I will push to begin restricting our offensive campaign so there is a 'managed reduction' in hostilities. Pao? Would you be agreeable to that proposal? And, how about you, Kruglov? What do you think?"

Pao spoke up. "I will agree to those terms."

Kruglov was more reluctant. "I will agree with Pao with the proviso that, if any of the remaining RVB targets fall within the Russian sphere of geographic influence, AND we are able to neutralize the *IWO* agents, AND avoid any detonations, then I will agree to a 'managed reduction' in force. But, until then, my forces will be pursuing *IWO* targets with a vengeance!"

Abbas thoughtfully responded. "You gentlemen have given me a tall bar to cross over. You are holding me accountable for the effectiveness of your own forces in locating and eliminating any remaining RVB threats. What if I give you exact information and you fail in execution? Is that my fault or yours? The scales seem somewhat imbalanced."

Even though he realized that Abbas was seeking more of an even accommodation, Arthur jumped into the conversation knowing that Abbas' statements would be received poorly by Pao and Kruglov.

"Abbas, the time for subterfuge and negotiation is over. I know that you feel these terms may be excessive, but we are dealing with the reality of having sustained massive destruction and untold deaths of non-combatant personnel.

No matter how you cut it, Aarzam went off the deep end when he began this conflict. And, as a result, I know that Clancy has already deployed nuclear weapons for possible delivery. I needn't tell you what that would mean to Muslim peoples worldwide. The fact that you have embedded your forces among civilian populations means a high number of civilian deaths resulting from multiple nuclear detonations.

The time for the détente-styled conversations you and I once enjoyed is over. We are now dealing with the realities of a major annihilation of Muslim citizens. In essence, the very people whom you sought to create a new country for will no longer exist."

Abbas considered Arthur's words. They had been well-chosen and to the point. And, while his brain raced to develop a counter-negotiation point, he could find none.

He looked over at Rasha who had been listening to the conversation, nodded his head, and pointed to a large folder on the table. Within were the details of the remaining RVB targets and the agents assigned to carry out the attacks. As she removed the information sheets from the folder, she recognized his signal to send the information to Arthur's email address.

"Gentlemen," Abbas said softly, "I will provide you the additional information requested. Arthur will receive it within the next five minutes, and he can then forward it to you."

Abbas paused. "This was not what I wanted, Arthur. I am attempting to regain control of *IWO* forces but, as you can imagine, I also have to deal with Aarzam's loyalists. This will not be something I can accomplish overnight. It will take some time to regain leadership over, what is now, warring factions."

Arthur felt as though a weight had been lifted from his shoulders. Finally, a door had opened toward peace, albeit some time off in the future.

"Thank you, Abbas. We'll be in touch." With that, Arthur disconnected the call with Abbas and returned to his two comrades on the phone. "Well, what do you think?" he asked.

Pao responded. "I'll call you back when I have neutralized the *IWO* operative in Beijing and Singapore. Right now, I have to go."

As Pao's line clicked, Kruglov chimed in. "I can see why you enjoyed speaking with him in the past, Arthur. But, my concern is for the other twenty RVB targets, the naval ships being lost, and the car bombs that are causing so much death and destruction. Like Pao, I have to see tangible results before I am willing to consider reducing our offensive actions against *IWO*.'

Arthur responded. "Kruglov, I am receiving Abbas' information now and am forwarding it to you. Good luck . . . I see a near-term target - Saint Petersburg - and a longer-term target identified as Moscow.

Kruglov's phone line clicked off.

3D.16 Changing R.O.E.

\* \* \* \* \* \* \* \* \* \* \* \* \* \* \* \* \* \* \* \* \* \* \* \* \* \*

Arthur stared at the wall map of the world. While Abbas' was his enemy, he had to admit that the *IWO* battle plan had been expertly conceived. Multiple, simultaneous attacks against a wide variety of targets was keeping the Western Alliance forces off balance. While the Alliance had superior weaponry, the need to provide emergency response assets to both combat the terrorist attacks was consuming valuable combat troops and equipment. Responding to RVB's, car detonations, ship explosions, and electronic bombs was severely taxing the civilian and military resources of the West.

After the loss of the ULCC *Lockerman*, the cruise liner *Norwegian Classic,* the warship *HMS Queen Elizabeth,* and the ULCC *Kellingsly* over the last several days, all Western Alliance naval commanders took rapid precautions to ensure their ships were free of *IWO* mines.

Unfortunately, the 'mine alert' was not distributed fast enough to prevent additional naval victims. It proved too late for the Chinese aircraft carrier *Liaoning* and the cruise ship *Esteem Princess,* both of which had succumbed to their damage in simultaneous attacks.

In addition, before all of the major warships could be checked, the *USS Harry S. Truman* (CVN-75) was targeted on the prior day. The only reason it did not sink was due to only half of the mines detonating. Since the pattern of detonation against the ship's hull was irregular, the *USS Harry S. Truman* was able to secure its watertight compartments and stay afloat. Propulsion was lost but the steam plants required for launching aircraft remained operational. Vengeance was on the mind of all of the *Truman's* flight crews.

Until Arthur could confirm a reduction in *IWO's* war posture, Arthur had to aggressively pursue targets regardless of their location. Accordingly, he modified the Rules of Engagement (ROE) to permit Western Alliance forces to attack all targets from which they we receiving fire. This ROE covered all *IWO* military targets as well as *IWO* targets-of-opportunity found within civilian population centers.

The fact that *IWO* was using schools, hospitals, churches, mosques, and government buildings as safe havens from which to launch attacks meant those installations would have to be neutralized, even if it meant civilian deaths. Arthur reasoned that if *IWO* saw that they would be attacked regardless of where they were located, they would eventually stop using these facilities, thus saving civilian lives in the long run.

It was a risk, but one that he had to take. *IWO* had 'attacked with a rifle' − Arthur was going to 'respond with a canon'. He felt the use of overwhelming force was the best way to shorten the conflict by exacting a terrible toll on *IWO's* forces. And, while he was intending to de-escalate the conflict with *IWO*, the short-term response needed to be swift and decisive.

His other dilemma was Clancy. He had to move quickly to remove him from exerting any authority over Western Alliance forces. An outright assault against Clancy's command center would be easily repelled by his loyalists. However, if he could lure Clancy into a trap, then his removal would be much easier and his loyalists could be defeated at the same time.

Arthur and the rest of his team boarded the Challenger 650. It was time to put his *IWO* counterattack plans into motion and stage Clancy's defeat.

# T+4 Day

## 4D.1 Danger in China

\* \* \* \* \* \* \* \* \* \* \* \* \* \* \* \* \* \* \* \* \* \* \* \* \* \*

Now having Abbas' information regarding the RVB attacks against Beijing and Singapore in hand, Pao moved swiftly to establish countermeasures.

Signaling to Chen through his office doorway, he issued his first directive as she quickly entered.

"Chen, get me the Northern and Southern Force commanders on the phone now! We have detailed information on *IWO's* planned RVB attacks against Beijing and Singapore!

With a shocked look on her face from having no prior knowledge of these specific threats, she momentarily hesitated.

"Chen! Now!" commanded Pao.

Chen quickly wheeled on her heels and sprinted to the communications center to establish the phone link with the two commanders.

In the meantime, Pao began composing an electronic communique to each commander, detailing the specifics provided by Abbas.

Chen quickly reappeared in Pao's doorway. "Sir, the commanders on are Line 1."

Pao picked up the phone receiver. "This is Pao. Have your communications offices bring you a dispatch I just sent with specific details regarding *IWO* RVB attacks being planned for Beijing and Singapore. Immediately deploy aerial and ground forces to intercept the attackers and take charge of the RVB's. You have nine hours to execute these orders. There is no room for failure. If either of those RVB's is detonated, you and your staffs will be terminated. Any questions?"

Although both commanders had been friends with Pao for over twenty years, the determination in his voice left no doubts as to the seriousness of the situation. "Yes sir!" was their emphatic response as Pao was hanging up the phone.

Pao had three things working in his favor. First, the size of his armed forces was significant, both ground and air forces. This translated to more "boots on the ground", more people that could be deployed to look for the target attackers. Second, China's extensive use of surveillance cameras provided a window into nearly every corner of Beijing and Singapore. Finally, China's recent launches of orbital surveillance satellites provided eyes in the skies that could supplement the limited images from the city-wide camera systems.

Just over four hours had gone by since Pao's call with the commanders when Chen knocked on his door. "Sir, we have video from both the Northern and Southern commanders. They've located their targets."

Pao rose from his desk and followed Chen to the conference room, which she had transformed in a bank of video monitors to capture images from a number of camera sources.

Two monitors were dedicated to satellite images, one dedicated to each of the two cities. Another set of monitors revealed camera angles from ground-based vehicles in each location. Finally, reconnaissance aircraft camera views were provided to aid in the search.

Focusing on each of the satellite monitors, Pao noticed that the target vehicles were identical makes and models. As if knowing what he was thinking, Chen spoke up. "Look, sir! They are using the same types of vehicles. If they have any more RVB's we need to track, looking for similar vehicles will hasten our search efforts."

\* \* \* \* \* \* \* \* \* \* \* \* \* \* \* \* \* \* \* \* \* \* \* \* \*

Given the lethal nature of the RVB, there was no reason to augment it with additional explosive material. However, the *IWO* agents in Beijing were competing with the agents in Singapore as to which team could create the greatest amount of death and destruction. While none of them would survive their respective RVB detonations, they craved the accolades that would be heaped on them by their fellow terrorists following their demise. To be exalted as a true martyr for the cause gave them the misguided hope in an eternal life of pleasure, in accordance with the tenets of their religion.

In Beijing, the three *IWO* agents thought the addition of fertilizer and diesel fuel would create an unforgettable explosion that would do far more destruction than the RVB alone.

This would be their undoing.

As police and military troops were conducting their aggressive search campaign to support Pao's orders, officials came upon multiple stores that had recorded sales of fertilizer to the same individual. In the same fashion, several fuel stations had noted substantial purchases of diesel fuel by the same individual. In addition, surveillance camera footage in all locations had recorded both the men and the rental truck they were driving. It was only through Pao's massive surveillance effort that the odd, multiple sales of fertilizer and diesel fuel were finally linked together.

By triangulating the multiple stores and fuel stations the *IWO* agents had used, Pao's intelligence team was able to narrow their search focus to a specific part of Beijing.

\* \* \* \* \* \* \* \* \* \* \* \* \* \* \* \* \* \* \* \* \* \* \* \*

In Singapore, the situation was eerily similar. Here, however, the *IWO* agents had decided to augment their RVB with Semtex, a general-purpose plastic explosive often used by terrorist groups due to its performance, ease of use, and portability. They were able to ferry the explosives from an Iranian freighter to Brani Industrial Park, where their staging area was located, just across the inlet from the Port of Singapore.

However, the ferry launch they used and subsequent loading of the Semtex into a waiting cargo truck was noticed by a harbor pilot who reported the oddity to the harbor master.

While the harbor master didn't think much about it at the time, it was only a few days later when he received the notification from Southern China Command alerting him to the potential terrorist activity in Singapore.

"We have a serious situation developing in Singapore!" stated the Army liaison officer on the phone. "Intelligence indicates a possible terrorist attack in Singapore by *IWO* operatives using a white, Isuzu 16-foot cargo truck with blue striping and a red cab. Contact us immediately if you hear of any information!"

The color of the cargo truck was unique since nearly all of the cargo trucks operating in the port were yellow, the color of the company that provided support services to all of the shippers.

"I did have such a cargo truck reported to me about three days ago, taking on cargo from a small motor launch. It was at the Brani Industrial Park, just across the bay from my office."

"Who reported this to you?!" demanded the liaison officer.

"One of my harbor pilots, who thought it unusual for a motor launch to offload cargo at a private boat launch" replied the harbor master.

"We are on our way. Have the harbor pilot in your office when we arrive in one hour!" shouted the liaison officer.

\* \* \* \* \* \* \* \* \* \* \* \* \* \* \* \* \* \* \* \* \* \* \* \* \* \*

Unbeknownst to the Beijing and Singapore *IWO* agents, they had been spotted by Pao's surveillance efforts. Abbas' strategic plan had called for all foreign agents to maintain an ultra-low profile to avoid attention and detection. However, little did they know that their lack of discipline in following his plan, by turning their missions into a game of outdoing one another, would result in all of their efforts being scuttled.

Back in Beijing, neighborhood surveillance cameras revealed unusual activity in an industrial park in the target sector of the city. A number of cars and trucks seem to be accessing a specific entrance and traveling to and from one building. Later, in the early evening, intelligence analysts monitoring surveillance cameras noticed a white cargo truck with blue striping and a red cab exit one of the buildings and leave the industrial park.

"That could be it!" exclaimed one of the analysts as he stood and pointed at the monitor. "Switch on the cameras for Zones 7, 8, and 9! Quickly!"

In unison, adjacent monitors were now tracking the cargo truck it stopped at a nearby gas station where the occupants exited the truck and began refueling. After ten minutes, the cargo truck departed the gas station and returned to the peripheral building in the industrial park.

"That's got to be it!" shouted the analyst. "Someone get Chen, immediately!"

After a few minutes, Chen returned to watch the replay of the surveillance videos while the analysts narrated their observations.

It was 9:00pm in Beijing – 8:00pm in Singapore – approximately twelve hours until the target detonation times prescribed by the information Abbas had provided to Arthur.

Chen raced into Pao's office. "Sir, we have confirmation on the location of each of the terrorist groups. I just viewed the video of the Beijing operation and I also received a text from a liaison officer in the Southern Command that they have the location of the Singapore terrorists."

Pao had been looking out his office window, taking in the beauty of the city panorama and wondering if he would be able to avert the two disasters confronting him. Upon hearing Chen's report, he smiled before regaining his stone-faced composure as he turned to face Chen.

"Well done, Chen. Tell both Force commanders to immediately intercept the terrorists with 'extreme prejudice'. Also, I want those RVB's recovered. Have the ordnance teams disarm the warheads and ship the bombs to Bunker 10 at our Beijing arsenal.

Chen hesitated. "But sir, don't you want to capture the terrorists for questioning?"

Pao's reply was short. "No."

## 4D.2 Danger in Russia

\* \* \* \* \* \* \* \* \* \* \* \* \* \* \* \* \* \* \* \* \* \* \* \* \* \* \*

*Saint Petersburg – GMT + 21 hours*
*Palace Square adjacent to the Winter Palace*

Kruglov was studying a city map of Saint Petersburg, looking at access routes to the target site provided by Abbas – the Palace Square.

The importance of this location was its proximity to the Admiralty, the Hermitage Museum, and the General Staff Building. The Admiralty served as the headquarters for the Russian Navy[8]; the Hermitage Museum was the former Winter Palace, the official residence of the Russian Emperors from 1732 to 1917[9]; and the General Staff Building housed the leadership of the President of Russia and his governmental departments.[10] It also happened to be the location of Kruglov's Saint Petersburg office.

Kruglov looked out of his office window across the Palace Square toward the Palace Bridge that crossed the Bolshaya Neva River. Abbas had chosen a great spot for a target. An RVB explosion in the Palace Square would not only kill most of the general staff, but it would also obliterate much of the Russian history defined by the Hermitage Museum.

The knock on his open office door interrupted his thought. He turned to find his communication officer, papers in hand.

"Sir, strategic and police forces in Saint Petersburg have been mobilized. We received a report from the Chinese that the terrorists in Beijing and Singapore used the same type of truck for transporting their RVB's. It was a white cargo truck with blue striping and a red cab."

"You think they'll use the same vehicle here?" Kruglov responded cynically.

It's how the Chinese caught them, sir. Maybe the terrorist cell in Saint Petersburg is following the same modus operandi."

"Fine" said Kruglov, almost reluctantly. "Add that information to the search intelligence we're providing to the security forces."

The communications officer turned to exit the room just as Menhinsky, head of the SVR, Russia's primary foreign intelligence agency, was walking into the office. They collided in the doorway, each intently focused on the papers each held in their hands.

After several apologies from the communication officer, Menhinsky finally entered the office and walked toward the map Kruglov had on the wall.

"I want you heading up this operation" Kruglov said dryly. "We have no room for screw-ups."

Menhinsky nodded. "We have some intelligence we're following up on."

Kruglov turned toward the window once again. "What do you have?" he asked, not expecting anything of importance at this time.

"We have a possible location of the terrorist cell" Menhinsky responded in a matter-of-fact tone.

Hearing that, Kruglov turned around quickly. "Where!"

Menhinsky tapped on the map. "It would appear our local security forces have been receiving reports of unusual late night activity occurring at the Gaskroft Petroleum Terminal located at New Port, southwest of downtown district, about 10km from Palace Square."

"Did they check it out?!" demanded Kruglov.

Menhinsky smiled. "They were more concerned by the fact that Gaskroft Petroleum is owned by the oligarch Yuri Gaskroft, who is a close personal friend of our president."

"I'll kill anyone who stands in the way of Russia reasserting its dominance in the world! Get your agents down there now and uncover what's happening! shouted Kruglov.

"I have agents standing by' responded Menhinsky. With that, he picked up his cell phone and dialed. "Execute" was the only thing he said prior to hanging up.

Kruglov looked at Menhinsky. You had people standing by? Why didn't you give the order yourself?"

Menhinsky smiled once again. "I wasn't going to send armed security forces onto Gaskroft Petroleum premises without my butt being covered. After all, we're not talking about some lowly city mayor or district representative. We're talking about Yuri Gaskroft!"

Kruglov smiled. "Ah, so you were using me as 'cover' in the event Yuri calls the president to complain?"

"You taught me how to play politics well" replied Menhinsky. As he turned to leave, he added "I'm heading back to the communications center. I'll keep you posted."

The sun was shining through Kruglov's office window. He looked at his watch - it was 4:00pm in Saint Petersburg. He turned his gaze out across the Palace Square and throngs of people making their way as though this was a day like any other day. Little did they know it might be their last.

As he turned back toward the map, he wondered how Pao was getting along in his search for the terrorists in Beijing and Singapore.

4D.3 Saving China

\* \* \* \* \* \* \* \* \* \* \* \* \* \* \* \* \* \* \* \* \* \* \* \* \* \*

Beijing – GMT + 16 hours
Singapore – GMT + 17 hours
identities, location, and their vehicle description

It was 9:00pm in Beijing – 8:00pm in Singapore – approximately twelve hours until the target detonation times prescribed by the information Abbas had provided to Arthur.

In Beijing, the IWO agents were making their final preparations for their morning attack on the Monument to the People's Heroes' in Tiananmen Square. With the final detonation wiring completed for the canisters of fertilizer and diesel fuel, they only had to arm the RVB and connect the master detonator for both. They decided to wait until tomorrow morning to complete this final task.

"So Taajwar," commented Haakim "do you think we will make a bigger 'splash' than Dahab and his team in Singapore?"

Taajwar took off his shirt and laid it over a chair. "I can't imagine them doing anything better than us!" Taajwar said laughing. "Dahab didn't do well when we were going through demolition training in Iran. He'll be lucky to even get his RVB to detonate on time."

Haakim returned the laughter and motioned for both to get some sleep. They took to their respective beds next to the truck, each leaving his AK-47 with reach. It was going to be a big day tomorrow and they needed a good night's sleep.

It was now 1:55am in Beijing – nearly five hours had gone by since Haakim and Tajwar had gone to sleep.

The industrial park where their staging building was located was bustling with rapid response troops under the personal command of General Choi, Northern Force Commander. Motioning silently to his commanders, the troops dispersed to surround the building. An armored personnel carrier (APC) fitted with a battering ram parked two hundred meters away from the garage door Haakim and Tajwar had used earlier in the day to fuel their truck.

Two of Choi's soldiers placed plastic explosive strips along the perimeter of the garage door, routing the detonator wires to the detonator located around the corner.

It was now 2:00am. At Choi's signal, the driver of the APC, started the engine and, putting it in gear, began accelerating to full speed toward the building's garage door. When it was one hundred feet away from the door, the demolition team detonated the plastic explosive strips. One second later, the APC careened through the door opening and skidded to a stop.

Disoriented from the door explosion and the stun grenades thrown into the interior by the rapid response troops, Haakim and Tajwar found themselves semi-conscious on the floor as the building filled with smoke from the debris.

Choi's troops quickly exited the APC and, combined with soldiers running in through the building's entry, all executed Choi's orders with 'extreme prejudice'.

One minute later, General Choi entered the building, his troops standing in formation around the lifeless bodies of the *IWO* agents. He stopped briefly to look at the bodies and then turned toward the truck to inspect its contents. Viewing the RVB surrounded by the canisters of fertilizer and diesel fuel, he stood silently, shaking his head. Choi reached into his coat for his cell phone, relishing the opportunity to inform Pao of the success of his operation.

It was 2:03am.

In Singapore, General Li, the Southern Force Commander, had been coordinating with General Choi to ensure their respective operations would be conducted simultaneously in order to prevent one set of *IWO* agents from warning the other of any interference from Chinese government troops. To achieve this coordination, General Li scheduled his assault against the Singapore *IWO* agents at 1:00am local time to compensate for the time zone difference with Beijing.

Beginning at 12:45am, and using the same tactics as General Choi, General Li quietly dispatched his assault troops around the remote warehouse in the southwest corner of the Brani Industrial Park.

Unaware of their having been discovered by Chinese intelligence, Nasir and Omar had been loudly arguing on how the Semtex was going to be wired for detonation.

"We need to have the Semtex on a separate circuit" argued Nasir, "so that it can be manually detonated by the driver. It should be used as a backup in case the RVB doesn't detonate on time!"

"No!" shouted Omar, pointing at Nasir. "They should be wired together to make sure both detonate at the same time! Your idea is stupid!"

Being older than the other two and having been placed in command of the group, Dahab finally spoke up.

"That's enough! Keep your voices down or you'll give us away!" Lowering his voice, Dahab continued. "We're going to wire the Semtex to the detonation circuit for the RVB; that way, they'll detonate at the same time. And to make sure, we'll wire a parallel circuit to the Semtex as a backup in the event the primary circuit fails. One way or the other, the RVB will go off. Now, no more talking – get to work – we're way behind schedule."

Dahab was irritable from lack of sleep and a recent text message from Taajwar in Beijing, chiding him for being behind schedule and questioning whether the Singapore agents would be successful in completing their mission at the Buddha Tooth Relic Temple in Singapore.

Dahab looked at his watch – it was now a few minutes before 1:00am. He was measuring lengths of wire when the muffled sound of a vehicle engine, off in the distance, captured his attention.

*That's odd,* he thought. *What would anyone be doing up at this hour?* He paused, deciding to put on his headphones before resuming his work. Maybe the music would keep him awake.

It was the music that kept him from hearing the sound of the APC's engine growing louder as it approached full speed toward the warehouse garage door. The explosion from the door being detonated and the subsequent crash of the APC through the now open door, caught the entire *IWO* team by surprise.

Within thirty seconds, Dahab, Nasir, and Omar lay dead. A Chinese demolition team began defusing the explosives in the rear of the rented truck.

General Li walked into the building to survey the scene. It was 1:03am. Time to call Pao with the good news.

It was 2:04am in Beijing when Chen's cell phone rang. The communications center had incoming phone calls for Pao from the Northern and Southern Force commanders.

Chen quickly walked toward Pao's office but stopped abruptly at his partially open door. Peeking through, she saw Pao lying on the sofa in his office, presumably asleep. As she quietly opened his door to alert him to the incoming calls, he opened his eyes and turned his head toward Chen.

"What news do you have for me" he said quietly.

"The Northern and Southern Force commanders are on your phone, Lines 1 and 2" Chen replied.

"Connect the calls and put them on the speaker" Pao replied dryly.

Chen conferenced the two calls together and announced them to Pao.

By now, Pao had risen and was slowly walking toward the office window. "What do you have for me gentlemen?"

General Choi responded "The *IWO* agents was killed at 2:00am this morning. The truck and its contents are being secured."

Without missing a beat, General Li spoke up. "Singapore is secure. The *IWO* agents were dispatched at 1:00am and their vehicle and its contents are being secured."

Pao slowly turned from the window. Chen could see the fatigued on his face and the lines of worry that etched across his brow from the burden he carried.

"Very well done, gentlemen. Very well done" was all that Pao said. With that, he disconnected the call and, turning toward Chen, said "Get Arthur on the phone."

4D.4 Saving Russia

\* \* \* \* \* \* \* \* \* \* \* \* \* \* \* \* \* \* \* \* \* \* \* \* \* \*

Saint Petersburg – GMT + 21 hours

Kruglov had just finished a late dinner with Tanya when his cell phone rang. It was 9:30pm in Saint Petersburg.

Menhinsky was on the other end of the phone. "We just heard from the Chinese. They took down both terrorist cells simultaneously thirty minutes ago. They recovered the RVBs and are moving them to a munitions bunker."

"Did they get any intel out of the *IWO* agents?" asked Kruglov.

"I asked," replied Menhinsky hesitantly, "but I got the feeling they didn't take the time to ask any questions."

"Sounds like Pao" mused Kruglov. "Where are we on our own search?"

"We haven't found anything yet" said Menhinsky. However, we do have three possibilities at the Gaskroft Petroleum docks at New Port. But, given who the owner is, I am a little hesitant to call for an assault on any of the warehouse locations. I think it would be politically astute for us to confirm the target before demolishing any of his property. Needless damage might have severe consequences."

Kruglov was getting annoyed. While he was also aware of Gaskroft's close personal relationship to the Russian president, he didn't particularly care for the man nor did he want to run the risk of the *IWO* agents succeeding in detonating their RVB.

"You can continue to search for more hours two hours. But, if we can't finalize the location by then, I want all three locations breached aggressively! If one turns out to be the correct target, then we'll have justification for assaulting all three. Just make sure one of them is the correct target."

"You're taking a risk" cautioned Menhinsky.

"No, the risk is yours" replied Kruglov. "You have been in charge of the search. You identified the terrorists' hiding location within the city; you identified the three possible buildings at the port; and you performed the assaults. I merely advised. Remember Menhinsky, when it 'rains', it flows downhill, and you're 'downhill' from me."

It suddenly dawned on Menhinsky that Kruglov would 'hang him out to dry' if the mission failed. It would be Menhinsky facing an angry Gaskroft and Russian president. "I understand" was all he could reply.

\* \* \* \* \* \* \* \* \* \* \* \* \* \* \* \* \* \* \* \* \* \* \* \*

Inside Building 401 at the Gaskroft Petroleum docks at New Port, Azim, Naseer, and Wasim were getting worried. There was still eleven hours to go before the RVB was scheduled for detonation at the Palace Square. Naseer had seen Russian soldiers patrolling the port earlier in the day and when he went out at noon for food, he saw that the number had increased dramatically.

"I am concerned that we will be discovered" said Wasim. "We should move the time for our mission up so we can ensure it is completed!"

"I too think we should move up the operation.

Azim looked concerned. This was the most important mission he had ever received from Aarzam in support of *IWO's* offensive actions against the Western Alliance. He couldn't afford to fail the responsibility that had been entrusted to him.

Finally, he responded to the anxious faces of his companions. "We'll move up the detonation time from 9:00am to 7:00am. If the Russian soldiers that Naseer saw at lunchtime are looking for us, we should still have enough time to complete our preparations. The other thing we will do is travel by water instead of by land. That should eliminate any potential confrontation with Russian ground forces."

Turning to Wasim, Azim continued. We'll offload the RVB from the truck to the trawler we originally used. Naseer and I will then travel up the Bolshaya Neva River to the Palace Bridge. Wasim, you will drive to the south side of the Palace Bridge and wait in the parking lot of the Peterhof Express building. Once you see us in a position approximately 500 meters south of the bridge, you are to drive directly up to the front entrance of the General Staff Building and detonate your cargo. If my calculations are correct, the RVB and your cargo truck should explode at about the same time."

Wasim looked confused. "Once we offload the RVB to the trawler, the truck will be empty. What am I supposed to do with an empty truck?!"

Azim smiled and motioned for the two men to follow him. They proceeded though a door connecting their warehouse room with an adjacent one. Once inside the new room, Azim walk over to several pallets of crates labeled "Farm Equipment". He took a nearby pry bar and used it to open one of the crates. Inside were neatly stacked rows of Semtex explosives.

Turning to the other two men, Azim waved his arm across the stack of crates. "We need to load all of this into the truck in the next two hours and complete all of the detonation wiring, including the dead-man switch that Wasim will have in the truck cab."

"Where did you get all of this?!" exclaimed Naseer.

Azim continued, turning slightly toward the pallets. "There are fifty, one-hundred-pound crates of Semtex . . . that's 5,000 pounds of explosive. Aarzam pre-positioned these explosives before we knew for sure that an RVB would be assigned to this mission. Given the potential of discovery by Russian soldiers, I am merely increasing our odds for success by providing the Russians 'two rabbits to chase' rather than just one."

Startled by this new revelation, Naseer and Wasim looked at one another in astonishment.

Azim just smiled back. "We don't have much time. Let's get going." And, with that, the men began their newly expanded mission with a greater sense of urgency.

\* \* \* \* \* \* \* \* \* \* \* \* \* \* \* \* \* \* \* \* \* \* \* \* \*

*IWO's* warehouse was located on the southern-most end of the port. Menhinsky's troops had started at the north end of the port and were working their way south, methodically checking every building to ensure no unnecessary damage would occur to Gaskroft's property. Even the lowest ranking soldier knew of Gaskroft's close relationship with the Russian president.

Menhinsky was surrounded by his senior staff, each in radio communication with different groups of the military detachment currently searching the port. The pace was slow because they had to search not only the buildings, but also the large cargo ships moored at the docks.

It was now 11:00pm, thirty minutes before the time designated by Kruglov for a multi-building assault in an effort to eliminate any possibility for the RVB to be transported to its designated target.

\* \* \* \* \* \* \* \* \* \* \* \* \* \* \* \* \* \* \* \* \* \* \* \* \*

Taking a break, Naseer sat on an empty oil drum while Wasim went outside to smoke a cigarette. They were sweating profusely from having transferred the 5,000 pounds of Semtex from the warehouse pallets to the back of the cargo truck. As they loaded Semtex, Azim completed wiring each of the 100-pound crates as they were positioned in the truck. Within a few minutes, the wiring was complete with a "dead man's switch" having been positioned by the driver's seat.

Looking toward Naseer, Azim bellowed out. "This is no time to relax! Get something to eat then get ready to leave. Where is Wasim?"

Naseer looked up wearily. "He went out for a cigarette. Besides, what's the hurry? We still have ten hours before the target time."

Walking slowly toward Naseer, Azim replied. "No, we don't! I told you guys earlier. I am moving up the detonation time to minimize our chance of discovery. With Russian security forces patrolling the area, we can't take the chance of being discovered by waiting until tomorrow morning."

Suddenly, the warehouse door burst open as Wasim ran inside. "We've got trouble!" he gasped and began quickly gesturing with his arms. "The entire port has been lit up, there security vehicles patrolling between the buildings, soldiers all over the ships and in the docks area - like ants swarming everywhere! And they're moving this way and getting really close!"

Azim quickly moved toward the door and, opening it just enough to peek outside. Menhinsky's troops were now within 200 meters of the IWO warehouse and slowly moving closer.

Closing the door quietly, he motioned for the others to come close to him. Whispering, he said "As I feared, we have run out of time! Wasim, you're leaving now!"

Pulling a map from the truck's cab, Azim continued as he pointed to the map with his finger. "Take the truck out of the south gate to the perimeter road, then head north! You have to get to the General Staff Building! At this hour, it should take you about twenty minutes! Leave now!"

With that, Azim shoved the map into Wasim's hand and pushed him toward the truck. "GO NOW!"

Turning toward Naseer, he continued as Wasim started the truck. "We have to get to the trawler – NOW!"

Azim and Naseer ran out of the south door of the warehouse and down a slight embankment to the trawler just as Wasim sped out of the building in the truck.

* * * * * * * * * * * * * * * * * * * * * * * * * *

Menhinsky was starting to worry. They had covered just about the entire dock area, including the freighters, and had found nothing. He was bent over, staring at a map of the docks when his staff's radios seem to come alive with chatter at the same time.

As he straightened up with a quizzical look, Colonel Rubodov stepped forward. "Sir, we are getting reports of lots of activity occurring at the far south end of the docks! A truck just sped off in one direction while people were seen running toward a fishing trawler moored nearby! The trawler is now moving north along the channel toward the Bolshaya Neva River!"

Menhinsky glanced at his watch – it was 11:03pm.

\* \* \* \* \* \* \* \* \* \* \* \* \* \* \* \* \* \* \* \* \* \* \* \* \* \*

Wasim was young and inexperienced. He didn't have the presence of mind to drive in a manner that would not attract attention. Rather, he was too excited at being put in charge of half of the operation! Consequently, as he began to daydream of the heavenly glory awaiting all martyrs to the cause, the cargo truck continued to speed along the darkened streets, attracting more attention than would be desired. As a result, the Russian security forces were able to easily identify the vehicle for interception.

Meanwhile, aboard the trawler, Azim and Naseer continued northward along the channel toward the Bolshaya Neva River. They had to make it to the Palace Bridge to cause the maximum amount of damage.

With the exception of the security lights illuminating the docks on their right, ahead and to their left was dark. Azim could only coax eighteen knots out of the trawler's old engine. Nonetheless, he began to relax at having made his getaway from the Russian troops that had been closing in on the warehouse.

He turned toward Naseer and clapped him on the back. "We made it! Azim shouted over the roar of the engines. "Tonight, I will see you in the glorious afterlife reserved for brave martyrs like us!"

Naseer's smile turned to a look of shock as he lurched forward, falling limp on Azim. As Azim instinctively wrapped his arms around Naseer's lifeless body, he felt the moisture of blood on the back of Naseer's shirt.

Just as he looked up, it appeared as if the entire dock area had erupted in gunfire, all being aimed at the trawler.

Azim ducked into the trawler's cabin and attempted to find cover as bullets ripped through the wood and shattered the windows. Laying on the floor, Azim reached up and began to move the trawler's steering wheel left and right, hoping a swerving target would be more difficult to hit.

After a long twenty seconds, the gunfire began to subside as the trawler moved beyond the range of the Russian's automatic weapons. Azim slowly rose to his feet. Looking behind, he saw that he had passed the Western High-Speed Diameter Bridge, which also gave the trawler cover from continued gunfire.

* * * * * * * * * * * * * * * * * * * * * * * * * * *

Colonel Rubodov turned from his radio to address Menhinsky. "We have the cargo truck under observation. It's currently heading east along the Western High-Speed Diameter Frontage Road. I have dispatched security forces to seal off all routes within a mile of the truck's position."

"What about the trawler that got away?!" asked Menhinsky. "What's the status?"

"We engaged it from dockside but didn't stop it" replied Rubodov. I have already recalled our air assets that were patrolling overhead in the Petrogradsky District up north.

"Assuming the RVB is either on the trawler or in the truck, we need to be careful on how we engage these targets" cautioned Menhinsky. "Instruct your people to disable the trawler and the truck by any means possible. We can't risk detonating the RVB because of careless use of force!"

Rubodov saluted and turned quickly to continue his coordination of forces.

Menhinsky continued with a final thought. "And get some of our patrol boats in the water to block the trawler from approaching the city center!" Rubodov waived in acknowledgement.

Now, all Menhinsky could do was wait.

\* \* \* \* \* \* \* \* \* \* \* \* \* \* \* \* \* \* \* \* \* \* \* \* \* \* \*

Wasim turned north on to Moskovsky Prospekt Road – in twelve minutes, he would be in front of Russia's General Staff Building. While disappointed he would not be able to detonate his explosives at the original target time of 9:00am, resulting in greatest number of Russian deaths, his mission would destroy the headquarters for Russia's top military leaders.

The flashing lights ahead caught his attention. As he looked around from the elevated roadway, he began noticing lots of flashing lights, all seemingly converging on his location.

Police cars!

As he looked further up the road, he could see that it had been blocked by several police cars. Beginning to panic, Wasim quickly looked at his map for an alternate route to the General Staff Building. He swerved to make a right turn down a narrow side street thinking he would outflank the police roadblocks.

But now, he was traveling east, away from his target. He had to find a way to return to a northerly direction so he could continue toward his destination. He made a quick turn to the left and saw that he would intersect with Ligovsky Avenue, a road that would take him north and place him just east of the General Staff Building.

As he made a right-hand turn onto Ligovsky Avenue, Wasim looked left over his shoulder to see that he had successfully bypassed the police roadblock. He smiled to himself and began to relax, believing he would now be successful in his mission. A final left turn on Nevsky Avenue up ahead would take him to his target.

He was only five minutes away from the martyrdom he so long desired!

\* \* \* \* \* \* \* \* \* \* \* \* \* \* \* \* \* \* \* \* \* \* \* \* \*

The trawler had left the channel and was now in the Gulf of Finland's sea inlet to the Bolshaya Neva River, the final route that would place him adjacent to the Peter the Great's Winter Palace. As soon as he passed under the Palace Bridge, he could detonate his RVB.

Casting a glance at Naseer's body on the floor of the cabin renewed his hatred for the Western Alliance. He would avenge the death of his comrade!

The trawler was now in the Bolshaya Neva River and only one mile away from his target. Azim set the autopilot for the helm that would keep him in the center of the river channel. He then turned to go down the stairs to arm the RVB and complete the wiring necessary for activating a Deadman's switch at the helm.

But as he placed his foot on the first rung of the ladder, the trawler was flooded with illumination from the approaching Blagoveshchenskiy Bridge as well as from several Hind Mi-24 helicopter gunships now circling closely overhead.

Azim scampered down the ladder and turned to run toward his deadly cargo. It was at that moment his world erupted in gunfire. Hundreds of rounds from all three of the Mi-24 gunships' Gatling guns raked the deck, the wheelhouse, engine compartment, and the waterline of the trawler's hull, quickly rendering it motionless in the water.

Azim was dead before he heard the first round fired.

As the trawler sank in the middle of the river, the lifeless body of Azim began to ebb and flow with the water now cascading over the railing. The tarp covered RVB soon disappeared from view as the trawler slipped below the surface.

\* \* \* \* \* \* \* \* \* \* \* \* \* \* \* \* \* \* \* \* \* \* \* \* \* \*

Menhinsky was lost in thought when Rubodov's voice startled him back to reality.

"We got the trawler!" shouted Rubodov. "It sank just southwest of the Blagoveshchenskiy Bridge in the middle of the river."

"Get dive teams out there now, see if the RVB was on board and, if so, let's get it ashore!" responded Menhinsky. "I want our demolition technicians to ensure it's been deactivated!"

Colonel Rubodov saluted and quickly wheeled away.

Menhinsky put his hand to his chin and thought *'One down and one to go.*

\* \* \* \* \* \* \* \* \* \* \* \* \* \* \* \* \* \* \* \* \* \* \* \* \* \*

Wasim was making his turn onto Nevsky Avenue, now only a little more than one mile away from the General Staff Building. As he accelerated out of the turn flashes of lights appeared all around him like fireflies on a summer evening. Having never been in combat, he didn't recognize the muzzle flashes from the automatic weapons sending a hail of bullets in his direction.

Sounding like hundreds of small hammers hitting the truck, the sound became deafening.

In a split second, the truck's windshield disintegrated. Wasim instinctively ducked but to no avail. Bullets were penetrating the truck's doors from both sides and he was caught in the middle.

The truck began jerking from side to side as the tires were shot out. Although mortally wounded, Wasim depressed the accelerator as far as it would go. Slumped over the steering wheel, he managed to keep the truck on the roadway for another half mile before succumbing from his wounds. As the truck reached the Anichkov Bridge, it veered to the right, rolling end-over-end down the embankment and into the Fontanka River.

* * * * * * * * * * * * * * * * * * * * * * * * *

"We got him!" exclaimed Rubodov as he was walking toward Menhinsky. The cargo truck rolled down the embankment into the Fontanka River by the Anichkov Bridge. I already have a recovery team enroute to deal with the situation."

Menhinsky smiled. While he relished the idea of reporting that he had defeated *IWO's* plan to wreak devastation in Saint Petersburg, he had to wait. Until the RVB was recovered, he wouldn't risk reporting prematurely.

He yelled out after Rubodov. "Colonel! Proceed directly to Anichkov Bridge and supervise the recovery of the truck. Let me know what you find. I'm going to the trawler site to see what the divers find."

\* \* \* \* \* \* \* \* \* \* \* \* \* \* \* \* \* \* \* \* \* \* \* \* \* \*

It was now 12:15am. Divers at the trawler site confirmed the RVB was onboard and that it had not yet been activated. They had secured it in sling and it as being raised to a waiting security ship.

A separate recovery team was at the Anichkov Bridge searching through the half-submerged cargo truck. Relieved in finding Wasim had not yet activated the dead-man switch, they began undoing the explosive wiring connecting the crates of Semtex found in the back of the truck.

At 12:45am, Menhinsky received radio confirmation that both sites were secure. However, knowing the potential fallout that would occur given that the *IWO* operatives had been using a warehouse on s property, he decided to leave the trawler site and proc Gaskroft'eed to the Anichkov Bridge to personally see that the site was secure.

Menhinsky arrived at the Anichkov Bridge at 1:15am. By now, a tow truck had pulled the upended cargo truck onto the shore. The rear doors were open as Menhinsky walked up to inspect the Semtex cargo. Receiving a 'thumbs up' from the demolitions team, he returned to his car. It was time to update his boss.

The phone ringing at 1:20am startled Kruglov, who had been in a deep sleep. Tanya stirred at his side. "Who is it at this hour?" she asked.

As he slowly came awake, he looked at the caller ID and recognized Menhinsky's phone number. Patting Tanya on her rear, he muttered "Go back to sleep".

He slowly rose to his feet and took his phone to an adjoining room. Stretching slowly, he finally answered the call on the seventh ring. "What is it" he asked, annoyed that he had been awaken from the first good rest he had had in some time.

"We recovered the RVB" Menhinsky reported. The *IWO* cell was using a warehouse on the docks owned by Gaskroft. Their apparent plan was to use a fishing trawler carrying the RVB and also a cargo truck pack full with Semtex. We sank the trawler and recovered the RVB. The cargo truck was stopped by the Anichkov Bridge and the Semtex has been secured. All of the terrorists have been eliminated and we didn't suffer any casualties."

Now fully awake, Kruglov smiled at his good fortune. "How close was it?"

Menhinsky hesitated before answering. "It was close. Based on the trawler's position in the river, I would assume their target was somewhere near the Winter Palace. As for cargo van, they were awfully near the General Staff Building. I assume that was a secondary target. If my assumptions are correct, then both were within few minutes of successfully completing their missions."

"That was close" Kruglov responded. "But, you did well, Menhinsky. Tell your team to take tomorrow off – they've earned a day of rest. I'll take care of briefing the president and dealing with Gaskroft. This incident should weaken his influence with the Central Committee."

Kruglov hung up the phone. *'That was too close'* he thought. *'Either the information he received from Arthur was inaccurate as to the detonation time, or the IWO operatives had moved up their operation because of Menhinsky's search operations.'*

Kruglov unconsciously shrugged his shoulders. Whatever the case, at least the worry was over. It was time to update Arthur.

# T+5 Day

5D.1 Dig Site Becomes Ground Zero

\* \* \* \* \* \* \* \* \* \* \* \* \* \* \* \* \* \* \* \* \* \* \* \* \* \* \*

The BM-21 rocket launcher was positioned behind some camouflage netting on a tramp steamer, three miles off the Israeli coast of Nahsholim, Israel. A modern variant of the Katyusha multiple rocket launcher used by the Soviet Union during World War II, the BM-21 held forty rockets that could be fired within twenty seconds to a distance of twelve miles.[11]

When *IWO's* first assault failed to overrun the archaeological dig site four days ago, Aarzam had made plans to attack the site once more with the intent of permanently disrupting the historical undertaking between Israel and Egypt. He could not fathom the idea of fellow Muslims working peacefully with their sworn enemy, the Jews.

His first response to the original attack at Nahsholim was IRGC's abduction of bus passengers yesterday – a great victory for *IWO*. Aarzam had been informed that, among the captives were several attractive college age women, some of whom were Muslim.

*Perfect* he thought upon receiving the news. *'If Rasha won't come to her senses, I'll just select one of them for my wife and use the rest as mistresses. Since I am the head of IWO now, I deserve such luxuries!'* Aarzam smiled at the thought of having multiple women serve at his disposal.

Now, the second response to the original Nahsholim attack was to be the rocket assault from the tramp steamer. *'There's no way Israel will expect this type of attack'* he thought. Aarzam was pleased with himself and smiled at the notion of being one step ahead of his adversaries.

He turned to his intelligence officer. "When does the dig site resume activity? We want to hit them when the site is full of people."

The intelligence officer responded. "Our informants have told us that the dig site will resume operations this afternoon. The Israeli military has been cleaning up the site from our first attack and has been installing defensive positions to guard against another ground assault."

"Excellent!" responded Aarzam. "We'll just fly our rockets over their positions, inflict mass casualties, and embarrass the Israeli's once again!" Aarzam began chuckling. "Tell the boat captain to launch his attack at 10:15am local time tomorrow. That should allow us to catch all of the archaeology personnel and their Israeli lackeys out in the open and achieve a great victory for our cause."

## 5D.2 Western Alliance Fights Back

\* \* \* \* \* \* \* \* \* \* \* \* \* \* \* \* \* \* \* \* \* \* \* \* \* \* \*

With the information previously supplied by Abbas on the details concerning the deployment of RVB's, Arthur, Pao, and Kruglov moved quickly to neutralize the remaining RVB terrorist cells. In each of the target cities, dragnets were established by local, state, and national law enforcement and security forces to locate and defeat the *IWO* terrorist teams seeking to unleash their RVB's against the Western Alliance.

While Arthur felt comfortable with the Western Alliance's ability to retrieve the balance of the twenty RVB's that remained on Abbas' original target list, there were still two RVB's, from the original twenty-five that were stolen, that remained unaccounted for. When would they show up?

While Arthur retained charge of strategic operations, the three men decided to divide the globe into three areas, thus allowing for a simpler chain of command for tactical command decisions. Pao became responsible for the Western Pacific, Australia, and eastern Asia. Kruglov held responsibility for Russia, Europe, Africa and western Asia. Finally, Arthur would control the Western Hemisphere.

While they were able to neutralize specific *IWO* threats, such as the RVB's, there was little Western Alliance commanders could do to counter the distributed threats such as the automobile and electronics bombs that were remote detonated by *IWO* operatives. According to Abbas' information, all of the bombs hidden within electronic devices should have been detonated within the last three days. However, news agencies were still reporting occasional explosions attributed to an electronic device.

As for the car bombs, 10,000 explosions had occurred over the last three days, leaving 50,000 car bombs yet to be found. Arthur's only course of action was to distribute a widespread bulletin on all news agencies for people to stop driving their cars and not to make purchases of any new ones. While that might cut down some of the deaths, remote-detonatable cars parked along streets could still deliver a lethal blow to those passing by. Although security forces conducted searches for the terrorists identified by Abbas' plan who controlled these remote detonations, the mobility of these *IWO* agents made their apprehension all the more difficult, especially since they were alerted to Arthur's preventive actions being broadcast by the news media.

Although reports of car bomb deaths continued to occur, the frequency of their occurrence began to slowly reduce. Unfortunately, while the rate of explosions dropped, the magnitude of lethality from a car explosion began to rise. *IWO* agents began secreting themselves in inconspicuous places so they could observe when the maximum number of people might be in the vicinity of a car bomb just prior to detonating their deadly weapon.

After a while, intelligence agencies began to see patterns in these explosions. By tracing each detonation, they determined which the make and models of automobiles were being used as weapons. With this knowledge, more specific alerts were now being broadcast over news media outlets, thus increasing the potential for civilian survival.

Arthur made contact with Admiral Torrey (Chief of Naval Operations) and Admiral Stephens. "Gentlemen, I want you to begin launching Alpha Strikes on all suspected *IWO* targets in your Operations Plan. I have watered down the Rules of Engagement (ROE) so your pilots and naval gunners will essentially be operating in a free-fire-like zone. This means any and all suspected targets are to be aggressively engaged, regardless of location."

"You know this won't play well with the politicians" replied Admiral Torrey. "They decry all civilian deaths that result from military action . . . always have."

"Let me worry about them" countered Arthur. "I have given the same guidance to Pao and Kruglov . . . and you know they won't hesitate to use this new ROE as a license to create a massive response against *IWO* for recent atrocities."

"But, there's one thing I want you to do for me. When it comes to making Sitrep's (Situation Reports) to Clancy, I want your communications to make it appear that your forces are in all-out pitch battles with *IWO*."

"That may be a little difficult" interjected Stephens. "Clancy is going to know that *IWO* has limitations on their weaponry. He sees them as backward, desert nomads. How do we get him to believe they have the ability to stop airstrikes, cruise missiles, or naval bombardment?"

Arthur continued. "Remember, *IWO* stole significant weaponry from the Russian and Chinese arsenals before this conflict began. For all we know, they have access to antimissile defense systems, portable radar installations for detecting incoming threats, and antiaircraft batteries for shooting down our aircraft. And, given that they are receiving direct support from the IRGC (Islamic Revolutionary Guard Corps), they have access to modern offensive and defensive military systems. Use your imagination. I need to create a scenario that confuses Clancy on the status of the conflict to entrap him and his supporters. It will be the only way to remove him from power."

"What about General Baxter's Satellite Command? Won't he be watching our progress from above?" countered Admiral Stephens.

Arthur replied. "I know the tracking paths of Baxter's satellites - I will send you that information. When you make your reports to Clancy, just select targets within your theater of operation that are outside the photo band covered by the satellites. That way, your real operations will be hidden from view. By the time they reposition the satellites for the prior strike, you will be reporting on a totally different one."

Admiral Torrey spoke up. "We can do this, Arthur. I'll get the word out to all Western Alliance naval forces. But what about the land-based air forces? Doesn't Clancy have them under his control?"

I've already thought about both the air and ground forces of the Western Alliance. Kruglov is a former Russian air force pilot and understands combat operations. Pao is a master strategist when it comes to the deployment of ground forces. I am having them coordinate with their counterparts in the Western Alliance to mask our intentions in providing phony reports to Clancy's command center."

"Sounds like a Rube Goldberg solution" Torrey jokingly responded.

"Maybe," replied Arthur "but that's where Butterman comes in. He will be the master coordinator, feeding you operational targets based on where the current satellite tracking is, to ensure your operations are not visible."

"But," continued Torrey, "how will this trap Clancy?"

Arthur continued. "I'm working out the details now – the plan should be ready sometime next week. That's why it's imperative the Western Alliance do as much damage to *IWO* over the next seven days as possible. We not only have to break *IWO's* back, but we also have to lead Clancy into believing he is winning a great victory so he'll let his guard down."

"Where does Abbas fit into all of this?" asked Stephens.

"I'm working with him as well" Arthur said quietly.

## 5D.3 Connecting with Abbas

\* \* \* \* \* \* \* \* \* \* \* \* \* \* \* \* \* \* \* \* \* \* \* \* \* \*

Arthur rubbed his chin. He was taking a big gamble working with Abbas. Not only was he the mastermind behind *IWO's* rise to prominence, Abbas was still the enemy.

Yet, Arthur had been successful in convincing Abbas to disclose valuable intelligence regarding the RVB's, the naval underwater mines, and the car bombs. That gesture of goodwill carried with it the promise of an eventual peaceful resolution to the conflict.

However, in the meantime, the Western Alliance had to keep up the pressure on *IWO's* forces. Kruglov, Pao, and he had agreed to a massive, short-term response that would break *IWO's* back, making Aarzam and his followers think twice about continuing the conflict. In addition, it would weaken Aarzam's command, thus making it possible for Abbas to regain control of *IWO* forces.

With these thoughts in mind, Arthur walked to the back of the plane. He had exchanged his Challenger 650 executive jet for an Argentinian Boeing 737 belonging to the Aerolíneas Argentinas, Argentine's largest airline. In the Boeing 737, he could file a flight plan that mimicked normal airline travel, allowing his aircraft to blend in with hundreds of other airline flights occurring around the globe, thus avoiding detection by Clancy's intelligence personnel.

As he settled into one of the numerous lounge chairs built for this corporate aircraft, he stared at his phone, contemplating the impending conversation with Abbas.

\* \* \* \* \* \* \* \* \* \* \* \* \* \* \* \* \* \* \* \* \* \* \* \* \* \*

Abbas was still depressed from the phone call he had with Arthur, Pao, and Kruglov two days ago. He had wanted so much to avoid a conflict with the West; yet, in spite of his carefully crafted back-channel discussions with Arthur, he had failed to prevent Aarzam from unseating him as head of IWO's forces.

Now, with Aarzam in charge of tactical operations, Abbas' desire for living out the remainder of his life in peace was quickly fading. It was time for him to become the warrior of his old days in Afghanistan. But, this time, instead of fighting the Russians, he would have to fight his own people - *IWO*.

Trying to devise a way to counter his own strategic plan that Aarzam was so astutely executing, Abbas' concentration was broken when Rasha suddenly entered the room. He had been so focused on regaining control of *IWO* and negotiating peace with Arthur that he had forgotten that she had arrived at his safe house two days earlier.

Wearing only a tee shirt and shorts, Rasha looked more like a westerner than a traditional Islamic woman. With her long, dark hair flowing across her shoulders and down her back, Abbas saw her more as a fashion model than a battle-worn desert fighter.

"Why don't you go put some clothes on" said Abbas. "This is my safe house, not some college sorority."

Rasha, now in the kitchen, flipped her long hair as she turned to face him. "Is there a problem?" she said coyly. "Most men wouldn't object to my attire."

Somewhat annoyed, Abbas responded. "First, I'm not most men. Second, I'm old enough to be your father. Third, I am more of a traditional Islamic man than you seem to give me credit for. And lastly, you're too young for me."

Rasha smiled and began to walk slowly toward Abbas. "You know what they say . . . the younger the woman, the sweeter the music."

"That's not what they say. I believe the saying is 'the older the violin, the sweeter the music'" Abbas retorted.

"Well, they have their sayings, and I have mine." Rasha reached down to place her hands on Abbas' arms and leaned close to his face.

For a brief moment, Abbas wished he were a younger man, taken in by Rasha's beauty and spunky personality. But, reality quickly returned. Abbas raised his arms slowly and gently pushed her away. "Behave yourself, little one. We have work to do to remove Aarzam from power . . . and it may cost both our lives before it's all over."

Rasha slowly stood erect. She saw Abbas as her ideal man and, although he was quite a bit older, she couldn't help be drawn to his strength and commanding presence.

As she turned back toward the kitchen, she replied over her shoulder. "We received a number of replies to your phone calls yesterday. Many of your old comrades from your Afghanistan days called back and are more than ready to stand by you to get rid of Aarzam."

Abbas perked up. That was the news he had been waiting for! With the support of his old comrades, he could mount a series of strikes against Aarzam's security forces with people who were familiar with his style of guerilla fighting.

Now, it was time to formalize a plan of action! But, just as he sat down at the dining table to begin studying regional and global battle maps, his cell phone rang. He looked over at the caller ID and saw Arthur's name appear.

\* \* \* \* \* \* \* \* \* \* \* \* \* \* \* \* \* \* \* \* \* \* \* \* \* \*

Arthur listened to Abbas' phone ring three times before it was picked up.

"Arthur," Abbas began. "It's good to hear from you. Was the information I provided of use to you, Pao, and Kruglov?"

Arthur hesitated before responding. While he wanted to work closely with Abbas to put an end to the conflict, he still had his reservations about Abbas' true intentions. He needed to keep

Abbas at arms-length. "The information is proving to be useful. There were some close calls in Beijing, Singapore, and Saint Petersburg, but devastation was avoided. We are now attempting to recover the balance of the twenty remaining RVB's. However, I am concerned that there are two RVB's yet to be accounted for. Do you know where they are and how we can eliminate the danger they present?"

Abbas felt somewhat sheepish. As finitely detailed as his strategic plan had been, he had allowed for some level of flexibility to counter any unanticipated actions by the Western Alliance. The remaining two RVB's fell into that category.

"My friend" Abbas began slowly, "I am afraid that I do not have that information. While they were originally kept in reserve in a warehouse in Bandar e Abbas, Iran, I don't know if they are still in that location, given Aarzam's current posture. I can provide you the address of the warehouse if that would be helpful."

"Please send it to the email address I am texting you now" Arthur responded. "It's a secure mailbox that I am using to receive communications."

Abbas motioned for Rasha to send the warehouse location to the email address Arthur was in the process of providing.

There was quiet on the phone for the next few minutes as the information exchange took place. As soon as Rasha sent the location to Arthur's email account, she signaled to Abbas with a "thumbs up" hand gesture.

"Arthur, you should be receiving the information momentarily" Abbas interjected.

"Wait for a moment" was Arthur's reply as he read the email just long enough to confirm its contents. He then immediately forwarded the information to Kruglov with a short note to prepare an airstrike since Iran was in Kruglov's area of responsibility.

"Okay" Arthur responded. "Let's begin a discussion on how we will get out of the mess we created through our mutual incompetence."

Abbas paused. While he first thought Arthur was insulting him, he realized that both he and Arthur's mutual weakness had been placing too much trust in subordinates with volatile natures. "I guess we did kind of 'step in it', didn't we?" Abbas replied.

"There will be plenty of time for recriminations later" mused Arthur. "Right now, we have a mess on our hands that needs a rapid resolution. But first, you need to know that Aarzam's recent actions have necessitated an overwhelming response against *IWO*. The Western Alliance is in the process of launching multiple Alpha Strikes against known and suspected *IWO* targets. Within twenty-four hours, I anticipate there will be a substantial number of casualties, both military and civilian, something I never wanted."

Although an old middle eastern warrior, Abbas knew a great deal about western battle tactics and weaponry. He knew that an Alpha Strike meant that all available Western Alliance aircraft would be launched to cause maximum damage against enemy forces within their respective theater of operations.

Nonetheless, Abbas felt he had to ask the question. "Arthur, is that really necessary?"

While Arthur understood Abbas' position of wanting to minimize Muslim deaths, he couldn't let Aarzam's actions of RVB explosions, sunken ships, car and electronic bomb deaths go without a severe response.

"Abbas, Aarzam started all of this. I'm going to finish it, one way or another." Arthur's tone was quiet but firm.

Abbas understood. Had an aggressor attacked his people without provocation, he would also want substantive revenge. "I understand, Arthur. You must do what you believe to be right. But, before this gets out of hand, we must construct a resolution to avoid any potential nuclear attacks or an overwhelming occurrence of suicide bombers."

"I agree" responded Arthur. "But our first priority is to regain control of our respective forces. That means your elimination of Aarzam and his supporters and my elimination of Clancy and his supporters. Once they are out of the way, we should be able to de-escalate the conflict rather quickly through a mutual drawing down of offensive forces."

"I agree" Abbas replied quietly. "We seem to have two battle plans that need to be created - one for the elimination of subversive forces and a second to coordinate the rapid drawdown of hostile activity. We should try to coordinate our respective plans for maximum effectiveness."

"I agree" responded Arthur.

Abbas continued. "Arthur, I believe the best way for us to accomplish this planning effort is to work side-by-side. I don't mean philosophically – I mean physically. We'll be able to coordinate in real time rather than over the phone or by computer and make quick, interactive changes as required. I would go so far as suggesting that we create our own combined command center from which all coordination of Western Alliance and IWO forces takes place. I know this sounds like a preposterous, revolutionary idea. But I feel it has real merit in quickly achieving our desired end result."

Arthur was taken aback. *Who had ever heard of two enemies working together, sharing intelligence, let alone working in the same command center?!* His silence was noticeable.

Abbas noticed the quietness on the other end of the phone. "I see my idea may be too radical for you. Maybe, you have a counteroffer?"

Arthur's mind was processing ideas in rapid fire succession. *While he could see the wisdom of Abbas' idea in its purest form, he couldn't get past the notion that they were still enemies. He couldn't forget that IWO was responsible for thousands of deaths in the last few days. And, while Abbas had not been in control of IWO's forces during that period, it did not change the fact that Aarzam was carrying out a strategic plan originally developed by Abbas. Nonetheless, he had met with Abbas in the past and those had been productive discussions. Could he trust Abbas once again?* His mind couldn't stop swirling around the pros and cons of a joint command effort.

"Abbas, I'll have to think about your idea and get back to you."

"I understand" Abbas offered. While he was disappointed that Arthur didn't readily embrace his novel idea for bringing the conflict to a rapid end, he also understood how radical his idea would seem to an enemy commander.

Arthur picked up the conversation. "Abbas, let me take the responsibility to get back with you tomorrow. In the meantime, I would encourage you to begin your planning effort as I will be doing the same. Let's see if we can come to some agreement on how we can coordinate our strategic plans for winding down this conflict in a manner that is mutually agreeable. Good-bye for now."

As he hung up the phone, Arthur remembered his former meetings with Abbas. Abbas was both professional and engaging and, were it not for the fact that they were on opposite sides of this conflict, he could easily see Abbas being a professional colleague.

But his first priority was to develop a plan that would result in displacing Clancy and his supporters from their current position of controlling Western Alliance forces. To that end, he made his way to a conference table in the center of the Boeing 737 and began looking at the multiple maps covering its surface.

\* \* \* \* \* \* \* \* \* \* \* \* \* \* \* \* \* \* \* \* \* \* \* \* \* \*

As Abbas hung up his phone, he glanced at Rasha who was staring at him with a "What did he say?!" look on her face.

"Well," Abbas began, "he didn't say 'no'."

"Why would he say yes?!" exclaimed Rasha. Your idea was crazy! He's the enemy, he's not our friend!"

Abbas took on his traditional fatherly tone. "Rasha, Rasha, Rasha. You must understand that, according to my sources, Aarzam has been faithfully carrying out the strategic plan I developed for *IWO*. A plan, I remind you, that was developed ONLY to serve as a deterrent posture against the Western Alliance, to pressure them into supporting our claim for a unified Islamic country.

I never wanted a war with the West. Our prior discussions with Arthur were meant to open a back door to formal negotiations to advance our cause. Now, with Aarzam's antics causing massive deaths in the West, we will be suffering a counterattack from the West that will result in the deaths of thousands, if not millions, of Muslims, both those affiliated with our military cause as well as innocent civilians."

Abbas slowly shook his head. "We have to find a way of unwinding this dilemma to prevent arriving at a 'point of no return', a point at which both sides find themselves unable to retreat."

Rasha walked across the room and sat on the couch next to Abbas. "I remember you telling me that before – that, you never wanted war with the West. I guess I never let it sink in . . . maybe because I have been a desert fighter for so long, I didn't think it was possible to ever have peace with infidels."

"Now, you're sounding like Aarzam" retorted Abbas. "Infidels? While that may have meant someone who didn't follow the Islamic faith in the olden days, it now has become an acidic synonym for insulting others of different faiths, like lighting a match next to a can of gasoline.

There are no infidels; rather, there are people of many faiths of which Islam is only one. Faith is an individual decision and, as history has shown, not one that can be mandated by a central government. Rasha, you need to broaden your perspective of others so that you will be successful in transitioning into a new society that will, hopefully, be available to us in the not-to-distant future."

It was at times like this that Rasha felt privileged to have personal conversations with Abbas. Hearing his wisdom caused her to become older and more mature in her outlook toward life. She leaned back in the couch and let her mind wander as to what life might be like in a new Islamic country where she could advance the cause of women's rights to parallel those enjoyed by women in Western countries.

## 5D.4 Regaining Control

\* \* \* \* \* \* \* \* \* \* \* \* \* \* \* \* \* \* \* \* \* \* \* \* \* \*

Of the original twenty-five RVB's secured by Abbas, Aarzam had deployed twenty-three, keeping two in reserve in the event targets-of-opportunity became available. Having used three against London, Brasilia, and Atlanta, Aarzam had twenty RVB's remaining in his arsenal, or so he thought.

Unfortunately, unbeknownst to Aarzam, Abbas' betrayal of *IWO* by providing the Western Alliance the locations of the remaining RVB's, would result in a significant degradation of Aarzam's plans to cause mass casualties.

As Day 5 (following the Predator attack on Harjiwan) was coming to a close, Western Alliance Forces had recovered sixteen of the remaining twenty RVB's. Covert operations by Western Alliance security forces were in the process of recovering the last four.

After some discussion, Pao insisted that a form of 'poetic justice' be applied against *IWO* forces, using the RVB's that had been repatriated from Aarzam's operatives as retribution for the destruction wrought upon the Western Alliance by *IWO*. While Arthur was concerned that such action would signal an unnecessary escalation in the conflict, Kruglov's fervent support of the idea caused him to withhold his concerns. He realized that both were attempting to save face from having been the original sources of *IWO*'s weaponry. They wanted 'payback'.

\* \* \* \* \* \* \* \* \* \* \* \* \* \* \* \* \* \* \* \* \* \* \* \* \* \*

With backing from Pao, Kruglov was nearly ecstatic at the prospect of using the RVB's against *IWO* forces. Although he had eliminated Serov, Andropov, and their associates for the loss of Russian weaponry to *IWO*, his pride still hurt from the damage that had been done to Russia's defensive posture while on his watch. In addition, he also wanted 'payback' against Iran for their bombing attack on his field headquarters located near Tbilisi International Airport in Tbilisi, Georgia.

Of the twenty RVB's that were re-captured or in the process of being secured, Pao had four, Arthur had seven, and Kruglov had nine.

As Kruglov finalized his target list, the following *IWO* locations rose to the top: Tehran (Iran), Bagdad (Iraq), Damascus (Syria), Sana'a (Yemen), Muscat (Oman), and Kabul (Afghanistan). Intelligence had confirmed these locations as being regional centers for *IWO* training, munitions storage, and troop billeting. Although major population centers, Kruglov felt that dropping RVB's in these locations would increase the magnitude of casualties among Muslim peoples. He reasoned that *IWO* was made up of and supported by Muslims, and didn't care if the death toll included civilians.

This still left Kruglov with three RVB's.

Kruglov now coordinated the air campaign against *IWO*. Making use of his heavy lift bombers, he instructed his munitions experts to load the re-captured RVB's for an aerial assault against his list of strategic *IWO* locations in the Middle

East. Hanging up the phone, he smiled at the impending disaster awaiting his *IWO* foes.

\* \* \* \* \* \* \* \* \* \* \* \* \* \* \* \* \* \* \* \* \* \* \* \* \* \* \* \*

While Pao had an affinity for infantry tactics, he couldn't resist the use of RVB's against *IWO* through the use of ballistic missiles. These missiles provided a better delivery system for the heavy RVB's, which couldn't be transported and deployed effectively using ground vehicles. Although Pao had access to the Chinese Air Force, they did not have the right type of heavy lift aircraft that could handle the weight of an RVB.

Like Kruglov, Pao looked for the most lucrative *IWO* targets in his area of operation in the Far East and Western Pacific. With only four RVB's at his disposal, he wanted to ensure he could achieve maximum casualties from their use; so, he was being very exacting in his target selection.

As he scanned maps of the area, Chen appeared at his door. "Sir" she said in a low voice, "I believe I have some information that may aid you in your target selection."

Pao motioned for her to enter his office.

As she approached the table of maps, she continued. "We have identified several sister organizations of *IWO* located in Indonesia. Our intelligence indicates that, while they are spread throughout the island chain, they have a concentration of senior personnel in Kupang, on the Island of East Timor. It is located about 1,000 miles east of Jakarta . . . here." Chen pointed at the map.

Chen continued. "A second target of interest is Sagoe. It's a small village on the northern coast of the Aceh province of North Sumatra, along the Malacca Strait. *IWO* has a large depot here responsible for distributing all weapons and munitions in Indonesia. It also serves as a disembarkation point for *IWO* troops.

We have a third target here in Zawtika, located in southern Myanmar, along the Gulf of Martaban. This appears to be the location of the regional headquarters that controls the movement of troops and munitions from the Chinese border to Indonesia. Their camp is only forty miles away from Yangon, which is the former World War II town of Rangoon, marking the southern end of the old Burma Road and extending north to Myitkyina. Our agents indicate that a great deal of supplies are being ferried along the old original road to *IWO* forces in Indonesia.

Finally, we have another logistics center in Torkham. It is a small town that sits on the border between Pakistan and Afghanistan. Iran sends all of its supplies bound for Indonesia through this logistics center. We have also learned that the Iranian munitions used against your field headquarters in Hotan came through this center on their way to Islamabad, where the Iranians had staged their attack aircraft." Chen paused to gauge Pao's reaction to the mention of this latest target.

Pao's memory was jolted back to three days earlier when his base at Hotan was attacked by the Iranian Sukhoi Su-24 aircraft. He rubbed his chin and smiled. It would feel good to strike back at both the Iranians and the logistics center that had provided the munitions for the attack against the Hotan installation.

"I like your target selection" Pao finally replied. "I want four missiles outfitted to each carry an RVB and be ready to launch within twenty-four hours. Be sure to coordinate the delivery of these weapons against the four *IWO* targets with General Li, our Southern Force Commander. Make sure his ground forces remain clear of these targets until after detonation to avoid friendly casualties."

"Yes Sir!" Chen wheeled about and left the office to begin coordination with Missile Command and General Li's headquarters.

Pao returned to his office window. A slight breeze arose, making the trees sway gently. As he let his mind wander, Pao was reminded of another time, when he was younger, and enjoyed life in the rural countryside.

As quickly as the thought entered his head, he relinquished it. *This was no time for daydreaming*, Pao told himself. Rather, it was time to unleash the might of Chinese and Western Alliance forces against *IWO* in the Far East and deal them a crippling blow.

Now was the time for a Western Alliance two-million-man ground assault against all *IWO's* territories comprised of Indonesia, Pakistan, Afghanistan, Turkmenistan, Iran, Iraq, Syria, Yemen, and Oman. *IWO* forces based on the African continent would be dealt with by Kruglov's air forces. This would be, by far, the largest ground military assault in world history.

Pao would make sure it was worthy of his name.

\* \* \* \* \* \* \* \* \* \* \* \* \* \* \* \* \* \* \* \* \* \* \* \* \* \* \*

Unlike Kruglov and Pao, Arthur decided not to use the seven RVB's he had recaptured. Instead, he elected to use conventional, precision-guided munitions whose lethality could be more effectively controlled. In so doing, he could maximize damage to *IWO* military forces while minimizing civilian casualties.

In spite of Clancy's tactical control over selected Western Alliance Forces, Arthur had been successful in subverting Clancy's command of Western Alliance naval forces under Admirals Smythe and Torrey. With these two in his corner, Arthur made plans to address *IWO* targets in his AO (Area of Operation) - the Western Hemisphere.

In North and South America, *IWO* was limited to independent terrorist cells located within population centers. For these targets, he relied on local and national police forces to carry out interdiction raids. Coordination of these operations would be left up to Colonel Butterman, Arthur's intelligence officer.

Arthur stood up from the table full of maps. He reached for his phone and placed a call to Captain Miller, Torrey's aide.

"Captain Miler, this is Arthur."

"Yes sir!" What can I do for you?" was the reply.

Arthur continued. "I need you to set up a conference call with Smythe and Torrey. Have them both in front of Western Hemisphere maps for a discussion on targeting. Let's set up the call to occur five minutes from now."

"I'm on it!" replied Miller.

As Arthur waited for the conference call to begin, he surveyed the Western Hemisphere map. *IWO* had two types of operations within his AO. The first were the terrorist cells operating within population centers that were to be handled by Butterman. But, the second were distinctive bases of operations, primarily located on islands adjacent to continent land masses in the Pacific and Atlantic Oceans. *IWO* had established these outposts for training, assuming that their remote locations would hide their activities and lessen the potential for discovery and assault by Western Alliance forces. It was these bases that would be ideal for surgical air strikes.

As Arthur stared at the map, his phone rang. "Arthur" began Captain Miller, "I have Admiral Torrey and Admiral Smythe on the line."

"Thanks", replied Arthur. "Good afternoon gentlemen. It's time we get to work."

"It's about time" chimed in Smythe. "Amen to that" offered Torrey.

Arthur continued.

> "Here's what I know at this time. Kruglov will be coordinating the use of Western Alliance air forces to launch attacks on *IWO* targets in Russia, Europe, and Africa. He is planning to use the RVB's he recaptured from *IWO* as part of his offensive strategy. I anticipate he will be launching a prolonged aerial campaign beginning tomorrow."

> "Pao is adopting a similar approach but primarily using a two-million-man ground campaign as a way of overwhelming *IWO's* ground forces. He also has some recovered RVB's and will be using missiles as his delivery platform. He is focusing on *IWO* targets in Indonesia, Asia, and the Middle East."

"Two million men!? Do you think Pao is trying to send a message!?" offered Smythe.

"How about Kruglov" interjected Torrey. "I get the feeling that he's going to bomb *IWO* back to the Stone Age."

Arthur responded. "While I was hoping to avoid a massive retaliation, *IWO's* global terrorist activities this past week necessitate a substantive response. My fear is that, once unleashed, this massive retaliation will be hard to put 'back into the bottle'. Once Clancy gets wind of this activity, he may decide to use our response as a catalyst for justifying the use of nuclear weapons. And, that is something we have to prevent."

"So, what do you want us to do?" said Smythe.

Arthur laid out his strategy. "I want to divide our naval forces into two offensive fleets – Atlantic and Pacific. Each will provide both aerial and cruise missile attack responses. Most of our targets are either island or coastal continental locations with minimal civilian populations. I am looking for precision responses to minimize civilian casualties."

"Don't we have some recovered RVB's of our own that we can use?" asked Torrey.

"We do" offered Arthur. "But, unlike Kruglov and Pao, I don't want to use them. I am looking for precision bombing against high value targets. Minimizing civilian deaths will go a long way toward the healing that will be necessary when this conflict is over. Unfortunately, I was unable to convince Kruglov and Pao of that position."

"Given the attacks they survived, it's personal for them" responded Torrey.

"It's personal for me too!" added Smythe. After all, I lost a lot of sailors when the *HMS Queen Elizabeth* went down a few days ago! I want payback just as much as Kruglov and Pao! But, as much as it pains me, I understand you taking the 'long view', Arthur. It will take a while to wind this conflict down and even a greater length of time to instill and era of peace between former enemies."

"Thank you, Smythe" responded Arthur. "I appreciate your understanding the challenges that lay ahead when the shooting stops."

Arthur continued. "Smythe, I'd like you to take the Atlantic fleet. Torrey, the Pacific fleet is yours. Butterman will send targeting packages to you in a few minutes based on the intelligence we have been able piece together. However, the target packages should be considered a minimally suggested list. I would encourage you to support your respective operations with reconnaissance flights to establish additional targets of opportunity. I want a massive response starting tomorrow and continuing for seventy-two hours. Each of your sorties should be considered Alpha Strikes – maximum aircraft utilization and cruise missile launches. Deal as much damage as you can within that seventy-two hour period.

"Why just seventy-two hours?" asked Torrey. Once we put them 'back on their heels', we should keep pressing forward."

"Two reasons" responded Arthur. "First, we will be running a parallel operation to remove Clancy and his supporters during that same period of time to prevent nuclear escalation. Second, I've decided to work with Abbas on a mutual de-escalation strategy. As I said, I must focus on the "long game."

"You still trust him!?" asked Smythe.

Arthur chuckled. "Well, I do. But, on the other hand, I don't see I have much of a choice. We must put an end to this conflict while, at the same time, leaving an opportunity for those remaining to see a future worthy of their interest and the pursuit of peace."

Arthur concluded. "Send me your battle plans tomorrow morning. I want to be able to monitor your operations so I can coordinate our other Clancy-related activities. Goodbye, gentlemen."

\* \* \* \* \* \* \* \* \* \* \* \* \* \* \* \* \* \* \* \* \* \* \* \* \*

Abbas knew that Aarzam was popular with the younger IWO fighters who had been persuaded by his '*IWO*-will-take-over-the-world' rhetoric. The idea of a fundamentalist, sharia-ruled global society appealed to them since it also meant their potential rise to governing micro-caliphates of their own. Because of this, the young fighters fought with abandon.

For those who erroneously elected to become martyrs in order to receive their promised seventy-two virgins when they arrived in heaven, Abbas felt sorry for them. Not only does the Quran not include this promise, there was still debate among scholars about the meaning of the words used in the hadith[12] which was typically referenced.

This meant that Abbas had to rely on his old Afghanistan comrades, those whom he had been able to convince during the meetings held at Murihajl Resort on the Island of Abd al Kuri five months ago. He had secured their support for long-term peace in exchange for success in persuading the Western Alliance to establish a single Islamic country officially recognized through a seat in the United Nations.

He needed their help now to overthrow Aarzam and his supporters, regain control of *IWO*, and begin winding down hostilities. Given their influence with their respective clans, they would be able to mobile a sufficient force to support Abbas' move to regain control of *IWO*.

As he contemplated who he would call first, his phone rang. Scanning the caller ID, he saw the call was from Sayyid.

While Sayyid was an IWO ally, Abbas had never fully trusted him. He, like Aarzam and Fathi, seemed to have plans for rising in *IWO* at Abbas' expense.

Hesitantly, Abbas answered the call. "Sayyid, what can I do for you?"

"Abbas, my good friend" began Sayyid, "I wasn't sure if you were still alive."

Maintaining his guard, Abbas responded. "What makes you think my health was in jeopardy?"

Sayyid continued. "Our compatriot Aarzam has been busy during the last few days. First, he led me into a trap at the Port of Sohar in Oman based upon intelligence indicating the Western Alliance was establishing a forward operating base for their general staff. When I got there, I was ambushed by a couple of gunboats – they didn't fare so well. Then, I heard that Fathi had been killed at an airport west of Sa'dah. So, when I heard that you were attacked in your home village of Harjiwan, I knew

Aarzam had to be behind all of it. All three of those attacks occurred within several hours of one another. That's too coincidental."

Abbas responded. "You are correct that my village of Harjiwan was attacked, but that was a missile strike by Western Alliance Predator drone aircraft."

Sayyid continued. "You're a careful man, Abbas. Did you ever think about how the Western Alliance knew you would be there? I subsequently found out that Aarzam leaked the locations of Fathi and you to intelligence agents for the Western Alliance. As for me, he tried to use his own soldiers but failed."

Sayyid paused. "We seem to have a traitor in our midst, my friend."

Abbas searched his memory for events from the last few days; however, a couple of those days were lost due his concussion and subsequent recovery from the missile blasts at Harjiwan. And, while he was aware of the ambition in Aarzam, Fathi, and Sayyid, the idea that Aarzam would assassinate all three of them was nonetheless surprising.

"To say I am shocked would be an understatement" replied Abbas. I had an inkling of Aarzam's ambition, not unlike what I observed in Fathi and you. But, to take out all three of us in one fell swoop is an aggressive move, even for Aarzam."

Sayyid was a little taken aback at Abbas' comment regarding his own ambition. He thought he had hidden his aspirations for

*IWO* well, but apparently, not well enough from the 'all seeing' Abbas.

Sheepishly, Sayyid responded. "Abbas, I won't deny having ambition, but it was never my intent to overthrow your leadership. You made some remarkable progress prior to Aarzam's theft of *IWO* leadership. I am calling to offer my support to your regaining control of *IWO*. What can I and my IRGC do for you?"

This was an unexpected surprise. Abbas had not been counting on Sayyid's support, primarily because he didn't trust him. But, Sayyid had access to Iranian aircraft that could prove useful in launching an attack on Aarzam and his followers. And, combined with Abbas' Afghanistan comrades and their forces, he might be able to mount a force that could overwhelm Aarzam. If he could time such an assault in conjunction with Western Alliance attacks, then Aarzam might be caught off-guard while he is focused on repelling Western Alliance forces.

"I would welcome your support, Sayyid" replied Abbas. "You have control of excellent military forces that, when combined with our experienced fighters from Afghanistan, should prove to be formidable. Put together a summary what military assets you have and how quickly they can be deployed. I will have our Afghan colleagues do the same. Let's plan on getting together to develop a strategy for removing Aarzam and his forces in two days. I will send you a location for our joint meeting."

"Sounds good" said Sayyid. "I'll await your call. Good-bye."

"Sayyid?!" Rasha called out from the kitchen as she made her way toward the couch with a drink in hand. "What did he want?!"

As Abbas laid down his phone, he responded. "Well, it appears that your paramour, Aarzam, has been a busy boy during the last few days."

At the mention of Aarzam being her paramour, Rasha mimicked a shocked expression on her face as she picked up a pillow and tossed it at Abbas.

"Abbas chuckled. "According to Sayid, Aarzam coordinated three simultaneous attacks a couple of days ago – one against Sayyid, one against Fathi, and one against me. Sayyid and I survived, Fathi didn't."

"Aarzam killed Fathi!?" Rasha exclaimed. "And he was behind the attacks on you and Sayyid!? I'll go and kill him myself!"

"Have patience, little one. Sayyid has agreed to support my efforts to oust Aarzam. And, when I combine his forces with our Afghan friends, we will be able formulate a plan that will result in Aarzam's downfall."

Turning more serious, Abbas looked directly at Rasha and pointed his finger at her. "And you," he paused "may end up playing a dangerous, but pivotal role in that downfall. But, for now, we have a lot of work to do to coordinate with our Afghan friends and fashion a unified army out of many independent tribes of fighters. It's time to build a coalition that will lead us toward our ultimate future."

Epilogue

**Stay Tuned!**

The world is in flames! *IWO* has been successful in executing a strategy of progressive, offensive strikes, each one more devastating than the former. No one in the Western Alliance is safe.

For its part, the Western Alliance has mobilized international militaries, recaptured RVBs, positioned nuclear weapons to overpower the threat posed by *IWO*, and is now poised for a massive counterattack.

For Aarzam and Clancy, total annihilation of the enemy is the only option.

But, how will Abbas and Arthur be able to prevent an impending global disaster? Will peace ever take hold once again? And if so, in what form will it take?

Join me for Book 4, *Two Images of God - Resolution*, the last book in our *Two Images of God* series, as we conclude this exciting story!

Publisher Information

**Like this book?**

If you like this author's work, your favorable review would be greatly appreciated at https://www.amazon.com/review/create-review?&asin=B0CZZ8JG21

**Other publications by this author may be found at:**

http://www.priatipub.com

*Languages of the World – A Multi-Lingual Introduction to Letters from Around the Globe – Volume 1* **[2017 eLit Gold Award for Education / Academics / Teaching]**

*Languages of the World – A Multi-Lingual Introduction to Numbers from Around the Globe – Volume 2* **[2017 eLit Gold Award for Children's Books (7 & Under)]**

*Languages of the World – A Multi-Lingual Introduction to Words from Around the Globe – Volume 3* **[2018 eLit Gold Award for Education / Academics / Teaching]**

*The Rest Areas of Your Life* with Study Guide

*A Practical Approach to Parenting*

*Two Images of God* – (Suspense Novel Series)
  Book 1 – *Quest* **[2018 Reader's Favorite Finalist]**
  Book 2 – *Discontent*
  Book 3 – *Conflict*
  Book 4 - *Resolution*

# End Notes

---

[1] https://en.wikipedia.org/wiki/Knesset
[2] https://en.wikipedia.org/wiki/Special_Service_Group
[3] https://en.wikipedia.org/wiki/Lingchi
[4] https://www.rei.com/learn/expert-advice/personal-locator-beacons.html.
[5]
https://en.wikipedia.org/wiki/Category:Guided_missiles_of_the_People%27s_Republic_of_China
[6] https://ctc.usma.edu/insight-into-a-suicide-bomber-training-camp-in-waziristan/
[7] https://en.wikipedia.org/wiki/Thermobaric_weapon
[8] https://en.wikipedia.org/wiki/Admiralty,_Saint_Petersburg
[9] https://en.wikipedia.org/wiki/Winter_Palace
[10] https://en.wikipedia.org/wiki/General_Staff_Building_(Saint_Petersburg)
[11] https://en.wikipedia.org/wiki/BM-21_Grad
[12] The 'hadith' contains traditional sayings traced with varying degrees of credibility to Muhammad.  The hadith typically referenced is number 2,562 in the collection known as the Sunan al-Tirmidhi.